"Nathan, want juice?" Harrison asked wearily

"No!"

"Banana?"

"No!"

"Sesame Street?" he offered recklessly.

"No!"

"A fully funded college account?"

"No!"

"Bad decision, kid. I'm a man of my word."

Harrison stepped over a diaper box, detoured around his rearranged furniture and surveyed the remnants of his living room. So this was the way parents lived. If he could bring order into the chaotic lives of parents, he was a sure candidate for a Nobel prize. Possibly two. They'd make a movie of his life. They'd erect statues in his honor. Children would be named after him. Political parties would court him. There would be Harrison Rothwell action figures.

Yes, life would be sw

Dear Reader,

I had fun remembering my two sons as babies when I wrote *The Bachelor and the Babies*. I have firsthand experience with most of Harrison's adventures, from the teething to the ominous cleanup announcements over the grocery store intercoms. And they say plastic mustard containers are unbreakable—ha! But stores love me now. The boys are teenagers and they still eat every two hours!

I hope you enjoy reading about mothering—from a man's point of view!

Best wishes,

Heather MacAllister

Heather MacAllister has written over twelve Harlequin Romance® novels as Heather Allison, as well as writing a number of Harlequin Temptation® books under her real name. From now on she will be using this name for both series. So, if you're looking for a sizzling Temptation or a rib-tickling romantic comedy from Harlequin Romance that will leave you breathless, all you have to do is remember one name: **Heather MacAllister.**

> *"Reading one of Heather MacAllister's romances is pure joy."*
> —Debbie Macomber

> *"Of course, she uses me for her inspiration."*
> —Linda Proch, Heather's college roommate

> *"It keeps her off the streets."*
> —Heather's mom

> *"If she's not going to clean her house, then I guess she'd better write books."*
> —Heather's mother-in-law

The Bachelor and the Babies
Heather MacAllister

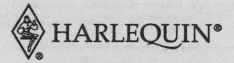

TORONTO • NEW YORK • LONDON
AMSTERDAM • PARIS • SYDNEY • HAMBURG
STOCKHOLM • ATHENS • TOKYO • MILAN • MADRID
PRAGUE • WARSAW • BUDAPEST • AUCKLAND

To Sandy Weider,
in gratitude for coming to so many autographings
over the years, and for carpooling to the meetings.
Now whose turn is it to drive?

ISBN 0-373-03513-6

THE BACHELOR AND THE BABIES

First North American Publication 1998.

Copyright © 1998 by Heather W. MacAllister.

CHAPTER ONE

"BUT I *have* to see Harrison Rothwell. Now's a good time for me. It'll just take a minute."

The insistent female voice vibrating through the closed door to Harrison's office sounded vaguely familiar, but not familiar enough for him to break off his telephone call.

Renewing his concentration, he closed his eyes and swiveled his office chair so that he faced the windows overlooking the flat vista of Houston, Texas.

"Now, Harrison, if we do take your *Rules of Time Management* back for a fifth printing, we'd like to tell marketing that a sequel is in the works."

"Felicia, I said all I have to say about corporate time management in that book. I already tweaked the chapter on fax machines and cellular phones and until we get widespread video phones, there's nothing further to add."

"Then how about something different?"

"What have you got in mind?"

His publisher drew a breath and Harrison visualized her gearing up for her sales pitch.

"Three words—*domestic time management.*" Felicia waited, obviously expecting a reaction.

Yes. Harrison had already toyed with the idea of expanding into the domestic market. Even now, clones of his time-management programs were cutting into his company's seminar and training business, however, it strengthened his negotiating position if

Felicia thought he was reluctant. He waited, letting the silence work for him.

"I *can't* make an appointment for later. I'll be sleeping later," sounded clearly outside his door. "Our schedules aren't meshing, here."

So much for working the silence. Harrison winced and covered the telephone mouthpiece hoping that Felicia hadn't heard.

What was that woman still doing out in his reception area? He was surprised that his assistant hadn't been able to evict the unwanted visitor. Sharon was usually very efficient in guarding Harrison's time from salespeople and the like. This person didn't have an appointment, Harrison knew, because he'd allocated ten more minutes to his current phone call, fifteen minutes to return more calls, then ten minutes to review notes before the Friday staff meeting. No appointments until after lunch.

"Don't you have anything to say?" Felicia prompted.

"Domestic time management?" he repeated, trying to ignore the arguing going on outside his door.

"*Yes,*" she insisted. "You've helped corporations desperate to increase efficiency with fewer personnel. How about some help on the home front? People are horribly overscheduled. Stress is king. Everyone is doing more and enjoying it less. They need downtime, Harrison. And you're the man to help them get it."

"It's a very tempting idea," he said slowly, as if he needed more persuasion. "Let me draw up some notes and—"

He was interrupted by a pounding on his door. "Harrison, tell your secretary to let me in!"

"Harrison? Is everything all right?" his publisher asked.

"Ah, let me get back to you, Felicia."

Disconnecting the call, he strode toward the door and flung it open. A woman with dark curls backed against him. He inhaled an unfamiliar perfume mingled with traces of cigarette smoke before setting her on her feet.

She whirled around, her hair flying. "Hey, Harry, how's it going?"

Harrison found himself staring into the defiant brown eyes of Carrie Brent, the nemesis of the White Oak Bayou Condominium Residents' Board—the same board of which he was a member. "What's this all about, Carrie?"

"I want to talk with you."

"Haven't you heard of the telephone?"

"I want to be able to see your face. It's harder to brush off someone when you see them in person. I learned that when I was a psychology major."

Harrison didn't want to hear about it. Psychology was the major Carrie quoted most often in her run-ins with the condo board. "Then you'll have to make an appointment."

"Well, I would if you had any openings when I'm awake."

He blinked. "You're awake now."

"That's what I was telling *her*." Carrie hooked a thumb over her shoulder, and shot a disgusted look at Harrison's secretary.

"Sharon knows that I have a very tight morning schedule, and you aren't on it, either awake, or asleep."

"This will only take a minute, unless you plan on being pigheaded and unreasonable."

Absolute silence was punctuated by the distant warbling of office telephones. Everyone within earshot of Carrie's voice was ignoring work to stare.

How often had Harrison preached keeping business and personal life separate? And standing in front of him, looking like an escapee from a gypsy camp, was Personal with a capital *P*.

"If you wish to discuss time-management techniques, then please make an appointment," he enunciated clearly for his employees' benefit. "If you wish to discuss anything not related to my business, then please contact me during evening hours."

"I *work* during evening hours!"

"And I *work* during daytime hours. You are interfering with that work." He turned to walk back into his office.

"Then I'll sit right here and wait until you take a break." She sank onto the floor outside his office, her skirt billowing around her.

She was making a scene. Carrie Brent was deliberately making a scene at his place of work.

She was wasting time. His time. His employees' time.

It was obvious that Carrie Brent was not familiar with effective time-management techniques. Harrison pointed to his office.

Carrie got to her feet and sauntered inside.

"Show's over," Harrison announced to the room at large, then firmly shut his office door. "You may have the six minutes left of the phone call you interrupted, which is five more minutes than you deserve," he snapped at her.

"How *generous* of you." Bracelets clanked as she dug into a shapeless sack that was apparently serving as her purse. She pulled out a crumpled, folded piece of paper. "*That's* where it went. Receipt," she told Harrison and continued babbling while she searched. "I bought these great hip-hugger jeans, but I was in a hurry and didn't try them on. They didn't fit. I couldn't believe it. I've been a size eight hoping to be a size six for as long as I can remember and the jeans don't fit! Then I realized they were from the petite department." She looked up at him. "I was *so* relieved when I saw the tag, you know?"

No, Harrison didn't know and he didn't want to know. He had to restrain himself from yanking the bag from her and dumping the contents on the floor. "You should have made an appointment. I don't allocate time to deal with disorganized malcontents."

"But you have time to cite me for—" she whipped out a folded piece of paper "—displaying hanging plants in unapproved containers?"

"Is *that* what this is about?" He didn't want to hear it. Carrie lived a lifestyle continually at odds with the conservative community at the condos. He didn't know why she insisted on living there, but she did, and the result was continual friction. "Make an appointment for an appeal to the board. I do not conduct personal business—"

"You and your appointments!" She waved the citation in front of his face. "By the time the board agrees to listen to me, the plants will be dead from lack of sunlight!"

"Not if you transfer them to approved containers."

"And approved would be white or green plastic?" She grimaced. "You people would prefer plastic to original pieces of Mexican pottery? We're talking *art* here!''

''White and green preserve the integrity of the outside appearance.''

She crossed her arms over her chest. ''Plastic integrity. I knew it.''

''Carrie...'' Shaking his head, Harrison shoved his hands into his pockets and leaned against the credenza. ''Those are the rules.''

''The people who wrote those rules have no soul. I'm trying to...to...'' She threw up her hands in frustration.

But Harrison knew exactly what she was trying to say. Carrie had lived in the complex longer than he had. He remembered the first time he'd met her. She'd arrived at his door with a pan of hot, vegetarian lasagna and a bottle of cheap chianti.

Since she lived on a downstairs corner, she'd watched the movers unload the few possessions that had survived the flooding at his former home. When she saw the secondhand couch and chairs, and the water-stained table legs, she'd apparently decided a soul mate was at last moving to White Oak Bayou Condominiums.

Harrison had enjoyed the evening too much to correct her impression.

But she figured out her mistake when Harrison had tried to repay her hospitality by inviting her to dinner after the decorator had finished replacing the furniture and changing the curtains in his new home.

Carrie had stepped inside the door, gazed around the room, then wordlessly stared at him with an expression he interpreted as betrayal. She'd handed him another straw-wrapped bottle, then left.

He'd never opened the wine, but he still had it. He didn't know why. Maybe as emergency fuel if his car ever ran out of gas.

"I didn't think my pots would bother anybody. Nobody can see them from the street."

"They are not approved containers."

"Pottery is better for the plants, anyway. Didn't anyone notice how *healthy* mine look and how anemic everyone else's look? Wait!" She smacked her forehead with the palm of her hand. "Plastic flowers! Of course. Has the board thought of that?"

"Carrie, this isn't the proper venue for your complaints." How could she think that coming here today and wasting his time would win his sympathies? Again, Harrison wondered why Carrie Brent wanted to live in a place where she so obviously didn't fit in. He made a show of consulting his watch. "Since I can't act without the rest of the board—"

"Can't, or won't?"

"Both."

They locked gazes. "In other words, I'll have to miss work if I want to challenge this citation," she said.

"If you're working at seven o'clock on the third Thursday of the month, then yes."

"And if I don't challenge it, then it goes into my file with all the other citations, until they reach critical mass, also determined by the board, and I'm evicted. Do I understand the plan correctly?"

Before answering, Harrison drew two deep breaths. It was a technique he found useful to keep from engaging in useless arguments. "I know of no plan to evict you."

Carrie looked at him as though he was as dumb as

dirt. "You know..." She held up the citation. "For anybody else, one of you would have knocked on my door, or left me a note telling me to take down the pots. But no. Because it was *me,* the board issues a formal citation." She jammed it back into her purse.

She was right, he had to admit. The board seemed to enjoy catching her in minor violations, such as when a car with her visitor tags parked in the covered area instead of the visitors' lot.

Or the fact that she'd set her recycling bin out too early because she didn't get home until after the morning pickup. When she'd petitioned the board, they'd refused to consider the fact that Carrie worked nights. Decent women shouldn't work nights unless they were nurses, one woman had said.

Harrison hadn't been on the board then, but they'd told him all about Carrie Brent when he'd been elected earlier this year.

Without Carrie, they probably wouldn't have anything to do, or anyone to discuss.

"Why do you keep fighting? Why not just move?" he asked.

"It's my home," she said simply. "I feel safe there and it's a great location. I used to live in a unit like yours with a roommate, but she got married. When the new owners converted the apartments to condominiums, I couldn't afford to buy the unit—I could barely make the rent as it was. Then they ended up with leftover space under the stairs and they offered to turn it into a one-room studio if I'd sign a five-year lease. So I did."

Harrison knew all about her lease. Why the condo board didn't just wait her out, he didn't know.

He held out his hand. "Give me the citation. I'll

tell the board I spoke with you, and that you will keep your plants inside."

"But how will they get any sunlight? Can't I just set them outside the door—"

"Carrie." He leveled a look at her and opened his office door.

She grinned. "Okay. Can't blame a girl for trying."

Actually he could, but he wasn't going to.

She sauntered—apparently her top walking speed—past him. "See ya around, Harry."

Harrison watched her stroll down the hall. "Don't call me Harry," he murmured under his breath.

Did she always have to make a huge issue out of everything? All the residents who lived at the White Oak Bayou Condominiums wanted was to maintain the property value of their investment. Was that such a bad thing?

"Was that business, or pleasure?"

Harrison glanced to his left, where his brother stood in the doorway to the office next to his. "That was trouble." He took the copies of the agenda for this morning's meeting out of Sharon's in-basket.

"Pity." Jon Rothwell watched Carrie's progress.

She'd passed through the glass outer doors, and was waiting for the elevator. When it arrived, she stepped inside and waggled her fingers at Harrison as the door closed.

"Can you *make* her business or pleasure?" Jon asked.

"*That* was Carrie Brent," Harrison said, irritated that she'd caught him watching her. He handed his brother a copy of the agenda. "It gives me pleasure not to have to deal with her."

"Oh, come on, you like her. You know you do."

"She's an irritating, disorganized flake."

Jon chuckled as he scanned the agenda. "Did it ever occur to you that she's causing all the trouble in order to have an excuse to see you?"

"I—" Harrison broke off. No, the thought hadn't occurred to him. He didn't want the thought occurring to him. He was sure the thought hadn't occurred to her, either. Pretty sure. "No."

Jon glanced at him assessingly and mercifully dropped the subject. "Under the vice president's report, do you want me to mention Felicia's idea for expanding into the domestic arena?"

"Felicia's already talked to you about it?"

"I'm marketing—of course she's talked to me about it, and I think it's right in line with our goals for the company."

Harrison didn't like being bypassed. "Domestic time management isn't that different from corporate time management. We have to consider the possibility that this venture will flop. People might feel ripped off."

Jon grinned at him. "You're a single man living in a condo with total outside maintenance, a maid and plenty of money. You have a five-minute commute. Try a wife, two kids, a dog and a huge mortgage on a house in the suburbs with an hour commute, and then tell me domestic and corporate are similar."

"It's a matter of—"

Jon held up his hand and disappeared into his office. "We've had this discussion before. In fact, *I* should write the book, not you."

"Be my guest," Harrison called after him.

"I would if I had any solutions."

Domestic time management. How hard could it be?

But Harrison had thought corporate efficiency was self-evident, too. The success of his company, Rothwell Time Management Consultants, proved otherwise.

People needed help managing their lives, and Harrison was delighted to provide that help. He felt a deep satisfaction when he received letters of gratitude from clients—and he always received letters of gratitude. Effusive letters.

He treated his talent as a calling and felt he was fortunate to earn a living at what he felt compelled to do.

His brother, Jon, didn't share that talent, but was an expert at selling others on it. Together he and Harrison were a great team. A profitable team.

Harrison didn't want them to become a stagnant team.

With that realization, Harrison knew he'd made his decision. Typically, he didn't waste time dwelling on it. Felicia had stewed enough waiting for him to call her back, anyway.

Harrison smiled to himself. Carrie Brent might have done him a favor by interrupting the call. Imagine that.

He returned to his desk, dumped the agendas beside the telephone and hit the redial. "Felicia," he said when he was connected with his publisher. "I've thought it over and I've already got ideas for adapting Rothwell's Rules for the home."

Though he didn't return any more phone calls before the staff meeting, Harrison felt the morning was well spent. Felicia made an offer on the project and Harrison would let her haggle details with the company lawyer while he ran the staff meeting.

The only blot on the day was the disconcerting lingering of Carrie Brent's perfume.

He stepped out of his office, leaving the door open in hopes that the room would air out, and stopped when he saw his assistant. "Sharon? You're not in the conference room?"

She sent him a tight-lipped look. "I'm sorry, Harrison. I'm waiting for a call from my daughter's teacher. It's a midterm telephone conference. I requested a telephone conference so I wouldn't have to take time off work."

"What do you call this?" Everyone who worked at Rothwell knew his position on conducting personal business during work hours.

"It's only for ten minutes. I arrived ten minutes early this morning. The teacher is obviously running late."

"But why should you and I have to be inconvenienced because she can't keep to her own schedule?"

"Some people are better at schedules than others."

It was an oblique reference to Carrie Brent. With her visit fresh on everyone's mind, he couldn't very well chastise Sharon, could he?

"Cecilia is covering the meeting for me until I can get there," she added.

"Join us when you can." With a curt nod, Harrison proceeded to the conference room, mentally plotting a chapter dealing with domestic responsibilities and how to plan for the unexpected.

Harrison didn't think his policies were unreasonable. In fact, they were the cornerstone of a successful business.

To him, it made sense that work should be completed during work hours and not at home. Home life should not interfere with, nor be discussed, at work. He felt just as strongly about the reverse—he didn't want company business interfering with his employees' family life.

Each employee received a copy of the company philosophy, which essentially maintained that if one worked efficiently and kept interoffice socializing down to a minimum, then all work should be able to be completed during a regular forty-hour week. If, due to unavoidable personal business, work was pending at the end of the week, then the employee could come in on the occasional Saturday. Never on Sunday. However, if the employee found that he or she was working most Saturdays, then that employee was encouraged to reevaluate his or her personal time-management skills.

Personal time-management skills. He'd assumed his employees would know how to translate the practices of the company to their personal lives. That's what he did. Obviously the moment *had* come for a book on personal time management. He knew others were out in the market, but they weren't based on Rothwell's Rules.

With a sense of mission lightening his mood, Harrison approached the conference room. People everywhere would be happier and more productive once he—

Jon stopped him in the doorway. "Hey, Hare, you got a minute?"

"No." Only Harrison's brother was allowed to call him "Hare," and not because Harrison liked it, either. If he let Jon get the occasional "Hare" out of his system, then he'd refer to Harrison by his full name in public.

"Let me put this another way, take the minute now and save time later, or I'll bring this up in my report and throw off the whole meeting schedule."

Harrison laughed. "Since you put it that way, what is it?"

Jon pointed to the seminars chart. "You've got me lined up to start the Chicago Manufacturing training next week. I can't go. You need to send somebody else."

Harrison's good mood evaporated. "What do you mean, you can't go?"

"Remember Stephanie's retreat?"

"Vaguely."

"She's leaving this afternoon, hooking up with some college buddies, then they're all going to tramp around the wilderness and prove they're Amazon women, or something."

Harrison tried to envision his sister-in-law going native and couldn't. This was a woman who thought "roughing it" was drinking beer out of the can instead of a glass. "I don't see the connection."

Jon gave him an impatient look. "The kids? Your nephews? I've got to be home to take care of them."

"That's what baby-sitters are for!"

"I'm not leaving them with a stranger for a week!"

"And when were you planning to tell me you were taking the entire week off?" The tone in Harrison's voice hushed the murmuring of the department heads gathered for the meeting.

"I'm not taking the whole week off. I'd planned to work at home. Make phone calls, reports, that sort of stuff. The kids have a play group thing that meets a couple of mornings and I'll stop by here then. And when I pick up and drop paperwork off, I'll bring them with me, or hire a sitter. I didn't see that it would a problem."

This wasn't a problem. This was a disaster. Harrison lowered his voice. "Chicago is a huge client. The contract was contingent upon you conducting the initial training."

Jon shook his head. "Postpone it, then."

"Impossible. They've had to rearrange the schedules of their top management to clear that week."

"Okay, offer them a discount and send somebody else."

"This is *Chicago Manufacturing,* Jon. They don't want discounts, they want you."

Jon glanced to his left and Harrison realized that everyone in the room was straining to hear each and every syllable they uttered. Here were the Rothwells, themselves, involved in a schedule conflict. How they handled it would demonstrate Harrison's methods better than any pamphlet printed with the corporate philosophy.

Trying to communicate all this, he stared into his brother's eyes. "What about Stephanie's parents? Can't they watch the boys?"

"They live in California."

"What about *our* parents?" Harrison didn't like the tinge of desperation in his voice.

Jon's face turned hard. "They live in Florida. I can take care of my own sons."

Harrison felt Jon was being deliberately difficult. "I know that. I only thought…well, whatever happened to doting grandparents? Wouldn't they like to visit their only grandchildren for a week?"

"I'm not asking them. Steph wants me to take care of the kids, and I'm going to. She's been at home with them ever since Nathan was born and she needs the break.''

"A break from what?" Harrison had been surprised when Stephanie hadn't returned to work. He was even more surprised that his brother hadn't objected. "They're two little kids. What does she do all day?"

Jon raised his eyebrows.

Murmurings from the female members of their audience told Harrison he'd erred.

He held up his hands, palms outward. "Sorry. I shouldn't have said that."

"You shouldn't have thought that," Sharon commented, slipping past them and finding her seat in the room. "But we all know you do."

Women were neither efficient, nor reasonable when it came to children. Harrison vowed to devote as many chapters to children as necessary in the *Rothwell Domestic Primer*. Ah, a title. That was a good sign.

Harrison carefully chose his next words. "What I *think*, Sharon, is that parents are reluctant to encourage efficiency in their children, and in the people who deal with children."

"Harrison, raising children is not like running a corporation."

Murmurings of agreement signaled mutiny in the ranks.

He forced a smile and casual body language. "Ah, but you see, running a household, even a household that includes children, is *exactly* like running a corporation."

"Uh, Hare?"

But anything his brother had been about to say was drowned out by the eruption of disagreement from the department heads—male and female.

Ah, skeptics. Harrison liked converting skeptics to his way of thinking almost as much as reading their subsequent letters of gratitude.

With a confident smile, he took his place at the conference table.

People quieted—except Sharon.

"You know how to run a corporation, but you don't know anything about living with children." Sharon had experienced more than her share of domestic crises lately. That must account for her inclination to challenge him today.

"You are correct," he said. The room hushed. "You all are also aware that Jon and I have been working out a schedule conflict. What we have here, are two problems with one solution. Backup plans are a key to avoiding delays. Jon, what's your childcare backup plan, say, for a family emergency?"

"*I'm* Stephanie's backup, then either of our folks."

"And after that?"

"Well...you, I guess."

Harrison smiled. "Exactly. Therefore, you'll go on to Chicago, and I'll take care of Nathan and Matthew."

"*You?*" Jon hooted.

"Yes. You'll keep the Chicago account, and I'll gain practical experience with children." Harrison addressed Sharon. "Do you think a week will be enough time for me to understand living with children?"

Sharon smiled. "A week will be more than enough time."

"Problem solved, then." Harrison felt a sense of satisfaction. "Shall we begin the meeting?"

CHAPTER TWO

"THIS is not a good idea," Jon said, and dumped the third load of baby paraphernalia just inside Harrison's doorway.

"Stephanie thought so." Harrison's sleekly contemporary entryway was no longer sleek. Neither was the kitchen, the spare bedroom nor the living room where he was now unfolding a playpen.

"How can you tell? She was laughing so hard when we called her, I know she didn't take us seriously."

"She does now." Privately Harrison attributed his sister-in-law's laughter to wine shared with good friends and the desire to appear indispensable. And since he was about to prove her wrong, he'd allowed her a few male-bashing cracks. He'd remind her of them when she apologized later.

He looked at his nephew—the mobile one. "We're going to have a great time this week, aren't we, Nathan?"

"Haht?" Nathan pointed to the window.

"Yeah, a hot time." Or Nathan could have said "What." Harrison wasn't yet fluent in toddler-speak.

Nathan toddled past him.

"I know Stephanie," Jon fussed.

Harrison noticed that Jon had only started fussing after he got married. In the interest of brotherly harmony, he declined to mention it.

"The only reason she agreed to you taking care of the boys is because she doesn't think you'll last more than a day. He—he*ck*, she didn't think *I'd* last more than a day.''

"Women like to think they're the only ones who can care for children." The playpen was bigger than it looked. Harrison shoved a chair out of the way.

"There may be something to that," Jon muttered. "Harrison, where is Nathan?"

"Right behind me."

"Hare! Pay attention. No, Nathan! Hot!" Jon leaped over the double stroller and snatched the twenty-month-old Nathan from under the lamp table. "Nathan likes electrical outlets," he explained.

"That's a dangerous hobby for a kid his age."

"You need outlet plugs."

"So, I'll get outlet plugs." Wherever those might be.

Jon still looked worried. "You know, you ought to come live at our house for the week. That's where all the boys' stuff is."

"And my *stuff* is here. I'll have more credibility with clients if I incorporate the boys into my own environment. I'll have a better understanding of what adjustments people who have children must make." Harrison was prepared to continue lecturing, but Jon was wrestling a squirmy Nathan into his high chair and obviously not listening to him.

"I never realized how much glass you have here," Jon called from the kitchen as he poured a few Cheerios onto the high chair tray. Nathan squealed and pounded the tray, bouncing cereal onto the floor where it rolled who knew where. "I'm going to buy furniture bumpers after I finish unloading."

Harrison didn't ask what furniture bumpers were, but imagined they weren't going to enhance the appearance of his once-pristine home. At Jon's insistence, he'd already removed the set of crystal coasters, fireplace tools, his collection of kaleidoscopes and anything sharp, breakable, or flammable. That pretty much cleared all surfaces three feet high or less.

Jon pulled open the cabinet beneath the kitchen sink and removed Harrison's cleaning supplies. "Store these up high, or get child safety latches for the cabinets." Looking around, he ultimately set the assortment of cleaners on top of the refrigerator.

"I'm running out of high places." Harrison put the pad in the bottom of the playpen and transferred a sleeping Matthew from his infant seat to the playpen. The baby was a sound sleeper. Good. They were going to get along just fine.

Jon walked over and stared down at his son. "He's a cute little guy, isn't he?"

He looked like a typical baby to Harrison. "Yes. Sure is."

Jon checked his watch. "This is a long morning nap for him, but it'll be easier to let him sleep until we've got everything settled. He was up in the night. If he gets cranky, don't worry. He's teething."

Harrison waved around the room. "Is this everything?"

His brother laughed. "Of course not. I haven't brought up their toys, yet. And there is a case of formula, diapers, the baby bath and a potty seat."

"Potty seat?"

"We've just started toilet-training, so don't expect miracles."

"I expect nothing in that area." Harrison didn't want to go anywhere *near* that area.

"At least Nathan will see it in your bathroom and

maybe get the idea.'' Jon shoved his hands into the pockets of his khaki pants. ''I'll bring up the humidifier, too, but I hope you won't need it.''

As he wondered where he was going to store everything, Harrison vowed to devote a minimum of one chapter in the *Rothwell Domestic Primer* to simplifying the amount of baby equipment insecure new parents had been convinced they needed. ''Who needs a humidifier in Houston?'' he wondered aloud.

''Parents with sick kids.'' After delivering that chilling piece of information, Jon left to bring up another load of the unending supplies needed to raise two small boys.

The instant the door closed, Nathan burst into tears. *''Daaa-deee!''*

''Hey, sport. Remember me?'' Harrison crunched on cereal as he entered the kitchen. ''It's Uncle Harrison.'' That sounded awkward, but Harrison was not going to be called Hare. Harry was not to be considered.

Apparently Nathan did not remember Uncle anybody and continued to cry.

Harrison poured him more cereal.

Still crying, but not as hard, Nathan ate a handful, then said, ''Joose!''

''Juice!'' Harrison repeated, his voice booming with false heartiness. ''The man wants juice.'' Trying to avoid stepping on cereal, he opened the refrigerator. ''We've got orange juice, tomato juice and beer juice.'' He looked over the door at his nephew. ''That's a joke.''

''Joose!'' Nathan smacked the plastic tray for emphasis.

Since orange juice seemed to go with the cereal

theme, that's what Harrison poured. He reached for a glass, then realized what he was doing and chose a plastic cup he'd bought at a Rockets basketball game. Who said he didn't have parenting instincts?

He poured a small amount of juice into the thirty-ounce souvenir cup and offered it to Nathan.

"Joose?"

"Juice," Harrison reassured him.

Nathan gleefully grabbed the cup with both hands.

"Need some help?"

"Nathan do it." He swiveled his body away and tilted the cup.

All the liquid rushed from the bottom of the tall cup to his face, startling him. He dropped the cup, blinked in surprise, snorted juice out his nose, then howled.

Harrison stared. With breathtaking speed, his kitchen, painted a fashionable white, with white tile and cabinets, had been splattered far and wide with dribblets of orange juice and pulp.

He picked his way to the paper towel dispenser and attempted to mop up Nathan.

That was the scene which greeted Jon's return. "Nathan," he called from the door, propping it open with a case of formula.

"Da-da!"

"Everything's under control," Harrison told him as Jon tossed in plastic bundles and boxes of diapers, which bounced and rolled over the couch. "We only spilled juice."

Jon walked over and stared at the mess. Bending down, he picked up the cup. "Is this what you gave him?"

Nodding, Harrison threw more paper towels on the

floor. Nathan had stopped crying, his interest caught by Cheerios floating in the orange juice on his tray.

Unfortunately Nathan's crying had awakened the baby, Matthew.

How could such a tiny person make such a loud sound?

"Nathan has a cup with a lid on it in the diaper bag. Use that," Jon suggested as he went to tend to Matthew.

"Now he tells me," Harrison muttered.

"Oh, and you'll have to strain the orange juice. The pulp clogs the spout."

The only strainer Harrison possessed was a cocktail strainer. It was barely adequate.

"You want a diapering lesson?" Jon asked.

"I can figure it out." Harrison spoke from the kitchen floor just as something dropped in his hair. His fingers encountered a squishy lump. Cereal. Or what used to be cereal before it absorbed orange juice. He looked up and caught Nathan shoving more over the side of his tray.

"I've learned a couple of diapering tricks that might make your life easier," Jon said.

"And other than keeping your children in a cage and hosing them down twice a day, that would be...?"

Jon laughed. "Don't think I haven't considered it. But seriously, don't leave Matthew alone on a table or he'll roll off, and keep him covered at all times."

"Why? He's not going to get cold."

"He squirts. And this kid has got an impressive range."

Harrison stood and peered over the kitchen bar. His

brother had unfolded a plastic pad and was changing Matthew's diaper on the floor in front of the fireplace.

Harrison had fond memories of other activities that had taken place on the floor in front of the fireplace.

He would never feel the same about that area of his home.

A knock sounded at the door. *"Excuse me?"* A grouchy Carrie Brent stood framed in the open doorway. "How's a person to get any sleep around here?"

Carrie, in her typically casual way, looked as if she'd rolled out of bed and climbed the stairs to Harrison's floor. She wore a giant gray sweatshirt with arms so long her hands disappeared into the sleeves. The bottom edge stopped a few inches above her knees and her feet were bare.

The contrast between the rumpled Carrie who stood in his doorway and the Carrie who'd come to his office yesterday was...interesting. Very interesting. So interesting that orange juice dripped from the paper towels Harrison held onto his running shoe before he realized he was staring.

"Most people aren't trying to sleep at noon on Saturday." He tossed the soggy paper towels into the sink and ripped more off the roll.

Carrie yawned, stretched her arms, and the hem of her sweatshirt rose. "They are if they work nights."

"So what do you do?" Jon asked over his shoulder after glancing at the silent Harrison.

"I review music groups at local clubs. And if a place is new, I'll mention the decor, tone and the sort of customers they're trying to attract. Anyway—" she yawned again "—after I get home, I've got to write the reviews. I usually go to bed about ten or eleven o'clock in the morning." Raking her hair back from her face, she padded into the room. "So what's all this?"

For some reason, the sound of a female voice had quieted the babies.

For some reason, the way Carrie casually manhandled her curls had quieted Harrison.

It was left to Jon to introduce himself. "I'm Jon, Harrison's brother. This is—"

"A baby!" Carrie had passed the couch and could see the front of the fireplace. Cooing, she knelt on the floor. "May I hold her?"

"Him," Harrison said, unwillingly reminded of the long-ago evening when he and Carrie had sat in that very spot and had eaten her vegetarian lasagna in front of the fireplace. "My nephews are visiting me for a while."

Jon handed a freshly diapered Matthew to Carrie.

"Aren't you just adorable? What's your name?"

"Matthew," Jon answered.

"Matthew, you're just a doll. A great big doll." Carrie's voice had gone all high and gooey as she repeated more nonsense.

But to Harrison's surprise, Matthew had stopped fussing and was smiling.

Something about seeing Carrie with the baby made Harrison want to smile, too. Matthew grabbed a handful of her dark hair. Carrie promptly retaliated by raising his shirt and tickling his tummy. The baby squealed.

Harrison grinned at Jon, only to find his brother regarding him thoughtfully.

Harrison guessed those thoughts concerned Carrie and whether or not there was something going on between them. "No," he mouthed.

"Why not?" Jon mouthed back over Carrie's bent head.

Because. Harrison knew there was a good reason— probably several good reasons. He simply couldn't think of them right now, not with Carrie looking all casually soft and approachable.

"Down!" Nathan had finished destroying his food.

Harrison, grateful for the interruption, removed the tray. Before he could set it on the counter, Nathan arched his back, slid down the seat and landed on the floor on his well padded rump. "Joose," he said and patted the floor. Then he picked up a stray Cheerio and stuck it into his mouth.

Harrison grimaced.

"Oh, yeah. I forgot to warn you about the high chair trick." Jon had arrived in the kitchen. "I also forgot the diaper pail. I'll snag one when I buy the plugs and the door latches."

Nathan got to his feet and ran toward his father. Jon picked him up. "You're wet." He pointed to the dark area on the front of Nathan's overalls.

"Joose," Nathan said.

"You can get going," Harrison offered. "I'll clean Nathan up."

Jon raised his eyebrows and grinned, setting Nathan on the floor. "Good luck."

Harrison had a feeling he wasn't referring to the kids.

Within moments, Harrison was alone with a half-dressed Carrie.

"Da-dee!" Nathan shrieked.

Okay, not alone.

Matthew had tired of pulling Carrie's hair and was puckering his face.

"Hey, Harry, I think he's hungry. Can I feed him his bottle?"

Bottle. Right. "Uh..."

Nathan escaped the kitchen and flung his orange-juice soaked body out the door.

Harrison ran after him and scooped him up before he reached the stairs. Then he kicked the case of formula inside his foyer and let the door slam shut.

"Da-dee!" Nathan made a full-body imprint of orange juice on the front door.

"And what have we here, Matt?" Carrie was bent over a diaper bag.

Harrison was so thrown off balance by the knowledge that he'd lost control of his house and the people currently within it, that he didn't even stop to enjoy the view.

Carrie stood and held up a bottle in a thermal container. "Should I heat it up first?" she asked.

"Uh, whatever," Harrison said as he wrestled a crying Nathan into the spare bedroom, tried to open his suitcase with one hand and keep Nathan from spreading orange juice with the other.

Eventually he succeeded in undressing Nathan, only to realize that all the diapers were in the living room.

He returned to the living room to find that all was quiet. Carrie stood in front of the windows, swaying slightly and feeding Matthew a bottle. She smiled at Harrison, all traces of her earlier grumpiness gone.

"You've done that before," Harrison commented.

"Actually, no." She looked down at Matthew. "But there doesn't seem to be much to it."

Harrison hoped there wasn't.

"Da-dee!" Nathan, wearing only socks, and damp socks at that, streaked by.

"Daddy's going to be back in a little while, sport," Harrison tried to reassure him. "Hang in there."

"But what are you going to tell him when Daddy doesn't come back? From the looks of this place, I'm guessing that they're here for more than the afternoon."

"I don't know," he admitted.

"Whatever you do, don't lie to him."

Nodding, Harrison picked up a box of diapers.

"Hey, Harry, those are baby-size. The toddler ones are in the purple bag."

Harrison squeezed the diapers in annoyance before exchanging them. "Please do not refer to me as Harry," he said, adding, "Harry and Carrie sounds like a vaudeville team."

She flashed him a grin. "I like it."

"I don't."

"Well, what do you want to be called?"

"Harrison."

"No kidding? I thought that was a name your mother saddled you with."

Tamping down his annoyance, Harrison corralled his nephew and the correctly sized diapers. "It was her maiden name."

Carrie raised her eyebrows. "Gotcha."

There was nothing to "get." Harrison liked his name just as it was.

Conscious that Carrie was a witness to his first attempts at undressing and dressing a tiny, uncooperative human—all prior humans had been more than cooperative—it took longer than he would have liked to get Nathan taped into his diaper and snapped into clean overalls. After two futile attempts to put his shoes back on—when had Nathan's feet turned to jelly?—Harrison decided to let the little boy run around barefoot.

And run was the operative word. Until Jon returned with the outlet plugs, Nathan couldn't be trusted to keep from electrocuting himself, so Harrison wasn't making much progress in unpacking the suitcase.

To Nathan, it was all very amusing to run squealing down the hall and watch Uncle Harrison lumber after him. Only Uncle Harrison was not amused.

Carrie was. He could hear her laughing. Okay, fine. Let her deal with the electricity addict. Harrison was going to unpack.

"Nathan, want to play a game?" he heard from the living room.

"Game," repeated Nathan.

"It's only for big boys."

"Game!"

"Can you take this bundle to your uncle Harry?"

Not Harry. Sure enough, Harrison heard Nathan's voice, "Hawee?"

"Yeah, you know, the tall grumpy dude in the bedroom?"

Harrison heard plastic crackling and Nathan arrived, carrying diapers. "Hawee?"

Knowing he was forever condemning himself to being called "Harry," or a version of it, Harrison mustered a big, "Thank you, Nathan! You're a big help. Let's build a diaper house under the window."

Though Harrison sounded as if he were the host of a children's television show, the little boy carefully set the diapers in the spot where Harrison pointed, then turned and grinned at his uncle.

That grin made up for a lot of the hassle, Harrison admitted to himself. He knelt down. "You little rascal, you've got the Rothwell smile, don't you?"

Nathan giggled.

"I know all about the Rothwell smile, so don't you try using it on me."

Nathan grinned wider.

"Rothwell smile?"

Harrison and Nathan looked up.

Carrie leaned in the doorway. "Oh, I see," she said slowly. "Yes, you've got the same smile. In fact, you look a lot alike. Both of you with those big brown eyes and your hair is almost the same color of brown, with the same little flecks..." She stepped forward and squinted. "Oh, that's cereal."

In spite of himself, Harrison laughed.

Carrie had a wistful expression on her face. "It's been a long time since I've seen you smile, Harry."

Harrison stood and Nathan ran down the hall. "I suppose it's pointless to ask you to call me Harrison?"

She stared at him for several long moments, then straightened. "I'll call you Harrison."

"Thank you."

"Hawee!" Continuing the game, Nathan was bringing another box of diapers to the room.

Harrison and Carrie exchanged looks. "Good job, Nathan," he said.

Carrie waggled her fingers. "Gotta go. Matt's in the playpen, but he's not going to be happy by himself for long."

Harrison walked her to the door. "Thanks," he said, knowing the word was inadequate.

"No problem. See you around."

They both nodded solemnly, knowing that when they next saw each other, it was likely to be on opposite sides of a hearing at the next White Oak Bayou Condominium board meeting.

Harrison thought the afternoon and evening went well, especially after he discovered which channels broadcast "Sesame Street." "Sesame Street" allowed him to install the safety latches without Nathan underfoot. Jon had wisely insisted in putting in the outlet plugs before he left.

Harrison bathed both boys, diapered them, gave Matthew his nighttime bottle, read the book *Goodnight Moon* and they were now asleep. Harrison wanted to join them, but decided to use the time to reclaim his living room and mop the kitchen floor.

He was surprisingly tired after his efforts, but all in all had no doubt that he could cope with two young children. Cope? He was doing better than coping. He was a natural. If he wasn't doing things in exactly the way his sister-in-law insisted, well tough. The boys were fine. In fact, he had several ideas to include in his domestic primer.

One of the sidelines of Harrison's business was designing products to go with his time management technique. Before he went to sleep, Harrison sat at his desk and sketched a piece of furniture, a sort of wall cabinet, with a place for all this baby equipment.

"The Well-Organized Baby" he called that chapter when he was finished outlining ideas for it.

Though it was one-thirty in the morning, Harrison felt extremely accomplished and self-satisfied when he turned out the light in his bedroom.

At three o'clock, he felt groggy and put upon. Matthew was crying.

Groping his way into the living room, Harrison turned on a table lamp. "Hungry, Matthew?" He bent down and picked up the baby, then squinted at the schedule Jon had left. There was nothing about a middle-of-the-night feeding. Maybe the long afternoon nap had thrown Matthew off schedule.

But Matthew didn't want a bottle. Harrison changed him, but that didn't help, either. In fact, since he had to go into the bedroom for diapers, he woke up Nathan. Fortunately Nathan was a trooper and immediately went back to sleep.

Matthew did not.

Though he hated to do so, Harrison called Jon at his hotel in Chicago.

"'Lo?"

Harrison didn't have to identify himself. Matthew's wails caught Jon's attention.

"Harrison is that you?" He sounded amazingly wide-awake. "What's happened? Is Matthew all right?"

"I don't know. That's why I'm calling you." Harrison explained the problem and everything he'd tried so far.

"Try this. Take your finger and press along his lower gums."

Harrison did and Matthew clamped down on his finger so hard, he yelped out a word neither of his nephews had any business hearing.

"He's teething," Jon said. "Stephanie lets him chew on a plastic ring she puts in the refrigerator. It might be in the diaper bag, but I probably left it at home."

"Gee, thanks, Jon."

"I'm sorry, Harrison, but I warned you."

Harrison gritted his own fully-erupted teeth and answered, "No problem."

By four o'clock in the morning, he was ready to admit failure. He was ready to grant unlimited parental leave to all employees with infants, because these people were obviously too deprived of sleep to function in the workplace. He also realized that he held the cure to the world's overpopulation problem right in his arms. After spending a day with a crying infant, any sane person would rethink the decision to become a parent. Those who didn't would be sentenced to a week in a two-bedroom condo with a toddler and a baby.

Harrison knew just the place.

He paced, more to keep himself awake than because it made any difference to Matthew.

Poor kid. At a time like this, a baby needed his mother. Just how far out in the wilderness was Stephanie anyway? Her group had only left Saturday morning. How far could a bunch of women hike in a day?

Over the din, Harrison heard a knock on the door. Great. Which of his neighbors had the baby awakened?

He looked down at himself. He was wearing loose knit boxer shorts, his usual sleeping attire. Clutching the baby to him, he peered out the peephole.

An eye peeped back at him.

Startled he jerked backward, which set Matthew off on another round of sobbing.

More knocking. "Harry—Harrison? It's Carrie."

"Terrific," he muttered to himself and flung open the door.

"What are you doing to the baby?" she demanded.

"I'm not doing *anything* to him! He's teething."

"*Ohhh*, poor Matthew. Come to Carrie."

She held out her arms and Harrison gladly relinquished his nephew.

Carrie headed for the couch, talking nonsense to the baby, and darned if Matthew didn't tone down his bawling to a few hiccuppy sobs.

Soon, even those subsided.

Carrie was an angel, an angel of mercy dressed in black leather, patterned stockings, boots and enough jewelry to lard a Nevada silver mine.

"He's exhausted," she whispered as the baby's eyes drooped.

Matthew wasn't the only one. "That's a trick. He does it just to give you hope, then snatches it away," Harrison grumbled. He lowered himself onto the chair by the sofa. Every muscle ached.

"You can hear him crying all over the complex," Carrie said.

"Did he wake you up?"

"Do I look like I've been asleep?"

Harrison took in the dark eye makeup and the way she'd bunched part of her hair on top of her head. No telling what she'd been doing. "You look like a corrupted doll."

She quickly looked down, but not fast enough to hide the flash of hurt in her eyes.

Harrison felt guilty for taking the verbal jab. "I meant...well, the contrast between the way you're dressed and the fact that you're holding a baby..." *Oh, give her the compliment.* "By the way, black leather is a good look for you."

She didn't look up, but she smiled. "I got home

twenty minutes ago and started writing up my reviews. Saturday is my busiest night.''

Matthew gave a shuddering sob, then wrinkled his face. Carrie reached for the bottle on the lamp table. ''Is this the one you were trying to feed him?''

''Yeah.'' How had she known he hadn't been able to get Matthew to take his bottle? ''He didn't want it.''

''Maybe he'd like a little now.''

Matthew latched onto the bottle as though he hadn't been fed in days. Within minutes, though, it was clear that he'd fallen asleep.

Harrison took him from Carrie's arms and put him in the playpen.

Together, they crept toward the door.

This was twice Carrie had helped him, and Harrison was uncomfortably aware of being in her debt.

He was also aware of other things, namely, that he was not wearing a whole lot of clothes and that leather really, *really* was a great look for her.

''Thanks for stopping by,'' he said, wondering if a kiss on the cheek might be in order.

''It's okay. I've got to get these pieces written and I couldn't concentrate with the crying.''

''Matthew was that loud?'' Harrison opened the door.

Carrie turned to face him. ''I could hear him through the ductwork. You know, you'd better be careful. You don't want to get crosswise with the condo board. I know from experience that they're very strict.''

''What do you mean?''

''I mean, Harry, that this is an adult-only complex.''

CHAPTER THREE

"HAWEE?" A small hand patted his face, barely missing his eye.

Harrison struggled back to consciousness, feeling as if he'd been hit by a truck.

"Hawee?"

"Nathan, buddy, what time is it?" Squinting at the digital clock-radio, Harrison groaned when he saw that it was 6:20 in the morning. At least he hoped it was morning. What if he'd slept all day?

He forced his eyes all the way open and turned on the radio. An organ blasted through the speakers. Church music. Sunday. Sunday morning.

He collapsed back onto the pillows.

"Joose?" asked Nathan hopefully.

"'S not time for juice," Harrison mumbled. "It's still sleepy time."

Nathan didn't argue with him. Seconds later, Harrison heard the crackling sound chubby legs wrapped in extra padded diapers made when they walked.

It grew fainter.

He wanted to go back to sleep. Desperately. This was prime sleep time, especially since he'd missed a chunk of his regularly scheduled sleep.

However... Rolling out of bed, Harrison followed Nathan.

The little boy was squatting by the playpen poking his finger through the net at Matthew's head.

If Harrison had arrived three seconds earlier, Matthew might have remained asleep. *That'll teach you.*

They all ate cereal for breakfast. Matthew's was a bit of unappetizing reconstituted white flakes, but he seemed to like it well enough.

Four hours later, Harrison was desperate for both sleep and adult company. It wouldn't be cheating to call one of the sitters on the list, would it? After all, if he had a wife, he'd be able to take a break. Harrison only needed a couple of hours. He'd go for coffee and read the paper. Shower and shave, even. So far, he hadn't because he wasn't comfortable leaving Nathan unsupervised.

Harrison called all three sitters. All three sitters were busy.

Even worse, they were busy tomorrow.

What kind of sitters were these? Harrison hadn't considered the possibility that at least one of the three wouldn't be available.

Who could he get to watch the boys? He didn't know any baby-sitters. Yes, he was sure there were professional agencies he could call, but Jon and Stephanie didn't want that and Harrison had agreed to play by their rules.

Okay, who owed him a favor? As he cut up chunks of banana for Nathan's lunch and watched Matthew's attempts to crawl, Harrison uncomfortably remembered the times he'd criticized employees for not having adequate backup child care plans in place.

That prompted an idea. Abandoning Nathan to his banana, Harrison recorded a memo to himself about establishing an emergency day care center for his employees. He wasn't about to get into the child care business, but if he stressed emergency, meaning short-term, and kept things simple, but licensed, he could see how employee efficiency and productivity would be increased.

As plans raced through his mind, Harrison became more enthusiastic about the entire child care issue. He should kiss his brother's feet for pointing out a weakness in the Rothwell time-management system.

Harrison became oblivious to his two charges, remembering them only when socially unacceptable smells from Matthew's diaper registered.

Resigned, Harrison checked on Nathan before cleaning up Matthew.

Nathan had squashed banana in his hair.

He'd also dumped it over the side of the tray and smeared it along the doorjamb. Harrison stared at him, then handed him more chunks. "Have fun." At least it would keep the little boy occupied.

He slipped on banana on his way out of the kitchen.

Nap time, blessed nap time arrived. Harrison took his long-awaited shower, then intended to try to find a baby-sitter for tomorrow, but it was so quiet and he was so tired...

Something woke him up. For once, it wasn't Matthew crying, though he was making noises. There was another noise that Harrison couldn't identify.

Nathan wasn't in his room. Fully awakened by the shot of adrenaline to his system, Harrison ran down the hall where he found Nathan. Matthew wasn't visible.

What was visible was a mountain of diapers, big, little and overnight-size, all mixed together inside the playpen.

"Matthew?"

"Matt in dare." Nathan giggled and pointed, but Harrison was already digging out his younger nephew. Fortunately the baby didn't seem upset at being buried.

Exhaling, Harrison sat on the couch and stared at the playpen, then at Nathan.

"Uh-oh," said the little boy.

"Uh-oh is right, buddy."

He couldn't get angry. Nathan had been bored, no real harm had been done and this was one of those situations Harrison might find funny in the extremely distant future.

"Go get the diaper box, Nathan," he said, not knowing if Nathan would or not.

"Game!" shouted Nathan and ran off.

"What have you got to say for yourself, Matthew? Did you feel like you were in an igloo?"

A drooling Matthew looked as though he couldn't decide whether he was unhappy or not. Harrison definitely wanted him happy.

"Hungry, sport?" Harrison spread out a blanket and set Matthew on it, dumped some toys around him, then retreated to the kitchen to make a bottle.

Nathan dragged a diaper box into the room. "Hawee?"

"In here, Nathan. Put the diaper box by the playpen." As he poured formula into a bottle, Harrison watched Nathan from the bar. The little boy stood without moving, then picked up the cardboard box and walked over to the blanket where Matthew was chewing on some rubber thing. Without warning, Nathan threw the box on top of the baby, who promptly started crying.

"Nathan! No! You hurt Matthew!"

The sound of Harrison's raised voice startled Nathan and he, too, began to howl.

But Matthew was Harrison's immediate concern. After checking and finding nothing more than a red mark on his head, Harrison tried to comfort him. "You're okay, Matthew. Come on, buddy, shake it off."

Nobody was shaking off anything.

Harrison wasn't at all surprised when he heard the knock at the door. He opened it without checking to see who was there. He just knew.

Carrie, or a version of Carrie, stood at the door. She wore a long, light-colored dress with a ribbon tied at the waist. Her hair was held back from her face with a band.

"I thought I'd come check on you on my way out."

"You mean you could hear us from the parking lot."

"Yeah." She grinned and walked past him.

Harrison eyed her getup. "You look like Little Bo Peep."

"And you look like, uh, heck. Real bad heck." She sat on the couch and patted the cushion next to her. "Hey, Nathan, what's the matter?"

As Nathan sobbed out his grievances against his uncle Hawee, Harrison checked his appearance in the foyer mirror. Yeah, he had a bad case of bed head caused by falling asleep when his hair was wet.

"Did you do that?" Carrie asked, pointing to the playpen.

Nathan nodded.

"He also beaned his brother with the diaper box," Harrison told her. Why did he sound as if he was tattling? "Would you hold Matthew while I finish fixing his bottle?"

"Sure."

As Harrison handed her the baby, he asked. "What's up with the outfit?"

"It's Sunday. I review gospel music on Sundays. Gotta fit in with the crowd."

"Don't you ever get a day off?"

"Mondays. The clubs are dark on Mondays."

Mondays. She had Mondays off. *She had Mondays off!*

Harrison walked back to the kitchen. He'd instantly decided to ask Carrie to babysit, but forced himself not to blurt out an impulsive plea. The trick was presenting his request in a way that would make her agree, while not making him appear desperate.

Because he was desperate. It was late Sunday afternoon and he was either faced with taking Monday off and losing credibility, or showing up for business as usual and demonstrating that *Rothwell's Rules* could be adapted to fit any situation.

Besides, the thought of grabbing a few hours in the company of adults made him giddy.

Carrie was great with the kids. Right now, she had Nathan stuffing diapers back into the box. They were even sorting them. Matthew had stopped crying and was watching.

"Are Matthew's teeth still bothering him?" she called.

"Why do you ask?"

"Well, I don't know anything about babies, but he's still fussing and he's drooling a lot." Carrying the baby, she walked over to the counter and started digging in the diaper bag. "I think I saw something in here when I was looking for the bottle yesterday. Yeah. This stuff.''

She pulled out a tiny box. Still holding Matthew, she read the side. ''For teething pain. It says to spread some of it on the baby's gums. Shall we do that, Matthew?''

Opening the box, she withdrew a plastic tube and squirted some jelly on her finger, then rubbed her finger on his lower gums.

Matthew screamed.

Startled, she and Harrison looked at each other. Carrie looked as if she was about to cry, too.

''What happened?'' Harrison took the tube.

''I don't know…did I use too much? Has it gone bad?''

Harrison squirted the jelly onto his finger then tasted it.

''Da—'' He swallowed the rest of the word. ''That stuff stings!''

''Let me see.'' Carrie repeated his actions. ''Ow!''

And right after the sting, the area the jelly had touched went numb. In Harrison's case, that meant his tongue.

''Awful tuff.'' No wonder Matthew was crying.

''Horubble.'' Carrie touched her finger to her lip. ''I wonduh how long it lath?''

Little Bo Peep had a lisp. Harrison started laughing. He couldn't help it.

''Id nod funny,'' Carrie said, but chuckled anyway.

''Okay, if you don't think that's funny, try this. I need a baby-sitter for tomorrow and I'm asking you.''

Her eyes opened wide and she gave a crack of laughter. Enthusiastic laughter. One might even describe it as laughter bordering on hysteria.

Harrison did not laugh. He didn't even smile. He finished making Matthew's bottle as Carrie, still laughing, sagged against the bar.

"Y-you're asking me to baby-sit for you?" She reached for the bottle.

"For Matthew and Nathan, actually."

"A favor, in other words."

"Call it a favor, if you like." A favor he was sorry he'd brought up.

"Oh, I like. What took you so long?" She'd stopped laughing and was gazing at him with an expression he didn't like. It was very much like the expression of someone entering negotiations in a very strong position.

Okay, so this would cost him. He was willing to pay. "What do you mean?"

"It was obvious to me from the minute I saw this sweet, little baby, that you were in *waaay* over your head."

Harrison resented that. "Because I'm a man?"

"Because you're you."

"Give me a chance. I'm not experienced with kids, but I'm learning fast."

Carrie gazed around the room. Nathan had stopped putting diapers back into the box and was sitting on the floor, surrounded by diapers in various stages of destruction. Sunlight from the window highlighted bits of fuzz that floated in the air, and from the white specks on Nathan's face, it appeared he was eating fuzz as a late-afternoon snack.

"Aw, Nathan." Harrison hurried to make sure his nephew didn't choke and rescue what diapers he could.

"I heard the crying, Harrison. Hours of it."

"Mine, or the kids?" he muttered.

She laughed. "I figured if I kept coming over here, sooner or later you'd ask me to baby-sit."

His back was to her. Harrison stared musingly at Nathan. She hadn't said yes yet. Nathan looked up at him and smiled. Ah, the Rothwell smile. It hadn't failed him yet. "Thanks for the tip, buddy," he whispered and swiveled to face Carrie.

"Okay, so now I've asked you." He smiled the Rothwell smile. "What's it going to cost me?"

"That's what I like about you, Harry. You cut to the chase." Carrying Matthew, she approached him. "I'll baby-sit for you tomorrow and in return, I want you on my side when the condo board meets."

"I already said I'd talk to them about the plants. I don't know what more you expect me to do."

"I want all my citations dismissed."

The Rothwell smile froze, then melted. "Carrie, I can't agree to that."

"Even if I'm right?"

"But you *aren't* right." Harrison stood. "The rules are clearly stated and you persist in violating them."

"Those would be the same rules that clearly state that this is an adult-only complex?"

"It's not the same. My nephews are only visiting."

"There are no provisions for underage visitors. This place is adult only. Period."

Harrison's voice was icy. "Are you threatening to complain to the board?"

"No, I'm showing you what it's like to be in my position. If the kids were visiting *me,* you know someone would complain, don't you? But because it's *you,* they won't."

She was probably right. Harrison gentled his voice.

"Why do you want to live here, Carrie? Why don't you move someplace where you can paint your front door red, hang wind chimes and Mexican pottery planters, and colored lights at Christmas instead of white ones?"

"I was here first," she maintained, looking down at Matthew.

"The place has changed since you moved here."

"I know. Once, it had charm. Then they renovated the charm out of it."

One of the selling points to Harrison had been the renovations to the plumbing, wiring and the resizing of the units themselves, not to mention the prime location. "I suppose we have different definitions of charm."

"The board wouldn't know charm if it bit them on their noses."

"With an attitude like that, it's no wonder you alienate them."

Carrie looked directly at him. "It doesn't matter what my attitude is. Haven't you figured that out?" She held his gaze for several moments before looking down at the baby in her arms.

He studied her as she swayed from side to side and murmured to Matthew. What about her rubbed those people the wrong way?

She was pretty, sometimes more than at other times, but never so spectacularly beautiful that she'd incite envy. She was friendly when given a chance to be. She didn't give wild parties. She wasn't wealthy, but she paid her rent on time. She drove an old car—another point of contention, but there was no legal way to compel her to replace it.

That had sparked the great oil leak debate, he remembered. Someone had accused Carrie's car of leaking oil and had produced oil-spotted paper he'd left under it to prove it. Carrie had defended herself with oil-spotted papers from cars driven by members of the board.

Except for Harrison's car, which had been leaking transmission fluid and he hadn't known it.

When he'd moved in, she had been the only resident to welcome him, other than the sterile letter accompanying the Residents' Agreement he'd received from the board.

He'd heard it said that the residents of White Oak Bayou Condominiums should project a certain image, and Carrie Brent was at odds with that image.

Truthfully he'd never identified with the liberal, vegetarian, supremely casual, everyone-do-your-own-thing image, either. He liked order and quality and, yes, rules. He liked expectations to be clearly stated because misunderstandings wasted time.

Still, had Harrison asked any of the "proper" White Oak Bayou residents to baby-sit his nephews? No, he'd asked Carrie.

And she still hadn't said yes. He tried the Rothwell smile again. "I'm only one of five on the board. I don't know what you expect me to do for you."

"I want somebody to tell the board to leave me alone! They're just trying to run up a bunch of citations so they can have me evicted. You can reason with them, I know you can."

She seemed absolutely convinced that Harrison was the key to solving her troubles with the Residents' Board. "I'll mention your situation, I can't promise results."

"Can you promise to bring my petitions to a vote?"

"A vote, yes, passing, no," he cautioned.

"Good enough." She beamed at him, demonstrating that she possessed quite a smile. "What time do you want me over here tomorrow?"

"You'll baby-sit?"

"Yes, but I'd appreciate it if you could get home by four o'clock. Monday is usually errand and laundry day."

Four o'clock? He'd have to leave the office early. Uncomfortably Harrison remembered all the times he'd criticized his staff for leaving early.

Of course the situations were in no way comparable. Harrison had had barely a weekend to adjust. Furthermore, he was hampered by being forced to follow guidelines set by the boys' parents. If Nathan and Matthew were *his* children, he'd have formulated his own guidelines.

"How about if you do your laundry here and I stay until five?"

"You've got your own washer and dryer?"

Harrison nodded, hoping he wasn't establishing a precedent.

"With a delicate cycle?"

Harrison had never used any setting with the word "delicate" in it. "I think so."

Carrie sighed blissfully. "And how soon may I start doing laundry?"

Harrison laughed. "If you're here by six-thirty, then I can leave for work early."

"Okay." She put Matthew's empty bottle on the counter and handed Harrison the baby. "You'll need to burp him. I've got to get going. Hey, Nathan, did you put away all the diapers?''

The little boy nodded his head vigorously.

Harrison opened his mouth to point out the diapers still littering the room, but Carrie spoke first.

''I see that Matt's are in the box, but yours go in this big-boy sack here.'' She picked it up.

''Big boy,'' repeated Nathan.

Carrie put one diaper into the sack and handed it to Nathan. He promptly stuffed another inside.

Carrie clapped. Nathan laughed and picked up another diaper. ''That's right!'' She watched a minute longer, then headed for the door. ''Bye-bye. I'll see you tomorrow!''

Harrison could hardly wait until tomorrow. In fact, he almost called her back.

Nathan did. ''Caweee!'' he screamed.

Feeling his patience slip away, Harrison closed his eyes, attempting to blot out the jarring pitch of Nathan's crying.

Think of climbing a mountain and reaching the top, he ordered himself. *See the view spread out beneath you...breathe the clean mountain air...find the serenity within—*

Matthew burped in his ear. Warm wetness spread over his shoulder.

''*Ca—wee!*''

''Nathan, want juice?'' Harrison asked wearily.

''No!''

''Banana?''

''No!''

'' 'Sesame Street'?'' Harrison offered recklessly.

''No!''

''A fully-funded college account?''

"No!"

"Bad decision, kid. I'm a man of my word."

On his way to the back bedroom, Harrison stepped over a diaper box, detoured around his rearranged furniture and eluded the stroller Nathan knocked over. When he got to the hallway, he turned around and surveyed the remnants of his living room.

So this was the way parents lived.

If he could bring order into the chaotic lives of parents, he was a sure candidate for a Nobel Prize. Possibly two.

They'd make a movie of his life. They'd erect statues in his honor. Children would be named after him. Political parties would court him.

There would be Harrison Rothwell action figures.

Yes, life would be sweet—once he had it organized.

CHAPTER FOUR

CARRIE had never looked forward to baby-sitting before, not that she'd had all that much experience baby-sitting.

She hadn't had all that much experience at anything. What she did have was a little experience at a lot of things.

It wasn't by design, or laziness or an inability to finish what she'd started. Carrie was the sort of person who threw herself wholeheartedly into whatever she did...until the moment when she realized it was the wrong thing for her to be doing.

Thus, after spending years in school, she'd dropped out without a degree because she'd changed her studies so many times, she'd never accumulated enough hours in any discipline to graduate. At the time, she wasn't concerned. Many people were late bloomers and she was obviously one of them.

But she'd wanted to bloom for some time now and had high hopes for her current job reviewing music groups and club acts. So far, she loved the nighttime hours and the loose schedule, wearing funky clothes and the interesting people she met. Maybe she'd never quite fit in with more traditional jobs and lifestyles because subconsciously, she'd found them too rigid and stifling.

She'd never pictured herself as a free spirit, but maybe that's what she was.

A free spirit. Carrie smiled to herself. She could practically feel herself blooming.

Now, if she could only find someone to bloom with.

With one eye on the kitchen clock, she gulped down the rest of her cereal and hoped Harrison was a coffee drinker. She was running just the slightest bit late. Not late, actually, but not as early as she'd planned.

Dumping her bowl into the sink, Carrie raced to her dresser and emptied the contents of the top drawer onto her bed. It was a luxury to have access to a washer and dryer that wouldn't chew up and bake her underwear and she wanted to take full advantage.

Grabbing all clothing in her closet that might possibly need washing, Carrie gathered her laundry in bundles made from her bedsheets and pillowcases and carted it upstairs to Harry's place.

Or Harrison, as he insisted on being called. She would try to remember, but she'd always thought of him as Harry and sometimes, it just slipped out.

She'd thought he'd had potential once. He was attractive, single and had a yearly income that allowed him to live in the White Oak Bayou Condominiums. Carrie didn't, of course, which was why she fought to stay in her little one-room studio. Anything else in her price range in this area wasn't safe.

But then he'd fixed up his place with all the personality of a model home, and she knew he was just another Condo Clone.

It still amazed her that she and Harrison could have spent an entire evening together without her realizing his true nature. She couldn't believe that the same man who'd sat on the floor laughing and drinking the wine she'd brought was the same impassive man she faced across the table at the Residents' Board meetings. Secretly Carrie thought the man with the casual smile and the well-worn jeans must still be around somewhere. Yesterday, with Harrison looking all rumpled and unshaven, she'd thought...well, she'd thought about the night before when he'd answered the door wearing Matthew and little else, that's what she'd thought about. Babies were a good look for him. There was just something about a man and a baby, she thought with a sigh.

And the fact that he'd volunteered to let his nephews visit for a week also put points in the good-guy column. She *couldn't* have been that wrong about him. Maybe he was burying his true self to comply with the White Oak Bayou image. Carrie bet she could loosen him up a little.

If she wanted to.

But whether she wanted to or not, what mattered now was that he was a member of the board who needed a favor and she planned to use it to her advantage.

So, just before six-thirty in the morning, she knocked on Harrison's door.

It opened almost immediately. "Good morning!" he boomed at her. He was fully dressed and his briefcase was by the door. Matthew was sitting in the playpen. There was no sign of Nathan.

Carrie laughed. "In a good mood at the thought of escape, or have you had too much coffee?"

He gave her a charmingly rueful smile. "Let's just say that I have a new appreciation for the role of parents and child care providers in our society."

Carrie grinned back at him. "I'll bet you do." She

set her laundry inside Harrison's front door, then smacked her forehead. "I forgot my laptop and I wanted to get some work done. Let me run get it."

He looked at his watch. "It's nearly six-thirty."

Oh, for ever more. "Will a minute or two make that much difference?"

"Actually, yes..."

Carrie didn't bother listening to him. By the time he finished explaining why every minute counted, she'd be at her front door. It had been a rhetorical question, anyway.

When she got back, Harrison was pacing. Matthew was beginning to fuss. "Have you fed him yet?" she asked.

"No," Harrison told her without the slightest compunction. "And Nathan isn't awake yet, but he should be soon."

In other words, Harrison was leaving all the work for her. Mentally Carrie shrugged. They'd be even when he had to start defending her to the board.

"You should see Nathan before you leave. He's probably feeling insecure with both his parents gone. If you just disappear, it'll upset him."

Judging by Harrison's expression, the possibility hadn't occurred to him. "How do you know?"

Carrie thought for a minute. How *did* she know? "I must have read it somewhere. But it makes sense. How about if you woke up and found some stranger baby-sitting you?"

"But he knows who you are. He screamed for you after you left yesterday."

"He did?" Carrie felt touched. Someone had missed her. Had anyone ever missed her before?

"Yes. You are now officially 'Cawee.'" Harrison

approached her with a sheaf of papers. "Here is the schedule I'd like you to follow today."

Schedule? Carrie read over the paper, then looked up at Harrison. "No mother wrote this."

"No, this is my schedule. Stephanie's isn't very detailed."

"It's probably detailed enough."

"Nevertheless, I want you to follow this schedule."

"Why? You didn't follow this schedule yesterday. I see nothing on here about diaper mountains and when I got here, there was a diaper mountain."

Harrison wore his remote face—the one he wore during board arguments. "Yesterday, I observed and gathered data."

Carrie made a face of her own. "I'll bet you did."

"And what I determined," he continued, "is that when children have no structure, nothing can be accomplished."

"Harrison, you've scheduled in diaper changes! You can't schedule diaper changes."

"I realize that, but they will occur and time must be allocated for them. I don't expect you to be able to adhere exactly to the timetable, but I do want you to record your actions, and the time they took to accomplish, on this paper." He handed Carrie a grid.

"Are you completely nuts?"

He stared down at her. "I can't formulate an accurate schedule if I don't know how much time to allocate to the tasks I want to accomplish."

"Speak English."

"I am."

Carrie headed for the kitchen. "Then I need coffee in the worst way, because you're making no sense to me."

Harrison followed her into the kitchen. "The coffee and filters are in this cabinet." After checking his watch, he got them out and proceeded to make Carrie a pot of coffee, talking earnestly, but quickly, about schedules and stress and parents and children.

Carrie leaned toward the pot and breathed in the aroma of the brewing coffee, hoping that her brain would absorb some caffeine.

He began to make sense, so it must have worked. "Wait a minute—you're one of those efficiency guys? The ones who tell you how to do everything faster?"

Harrison looked pained. "In the most simplistic terms, yes."

"Cool."

"I've, ah, been asked to write a book on domestic time management."

"Real cool."

"So I'm using my nephews' visit to familiarize myself with the special needs of working parents."

Enough coffee had dripped into the pot for Carrie to pour herself half a cup. "Sugar?"

Silently Harrison placed the sugar bowl on the counter, along with a spoon. Carrie added two spoonfuls and watched him grimace. She stuck her cup under the faucet and added enough water to cool the coffee, then drained the entire cup.

"How can you drink it that way?" he exclaimed, sounding more human than he had for the past several minutes.

"I didn't want to burn my tongue." She leaned against the counter. "Okay, the old brain is working now and it says that you are going merrily off to manage other people's time and are leaving me to do all your research."

Harrison took her cup from her. "No more coffee. I like you better asleep and malleable."

That surprised a laugh out of her. "I'm right, aren't I?"

"You would be helping me with my research, yes."

"So I'm not just a mere baby-sitter."

Further surprising her, he said, "I've never thought of you as a mere anything."

While she blinked at him, he reached for the schedule and handed it to her. "By the way, if you start feeling like this is too much trouble, remind yourself that the planter citation you just got is your tenth."

She snatched the schedule from him, mumbling, "I wondered when you would realize that."

"Ten strikes and you're out, right?" He was referring to the eviction policy.

Carrie glared at him. "Okay, I'll follow your stupid schedule. Now go!" She made shooing motions. "I've got a baby to feed." She went over to the playpen and picked up Matthew. "Don't forget to say goodbye to Nathan."

"Are you sure you want me to wake him up?"

"Too late." Carrie pointed behind Harrison.

"Hawee?" Nathan trotted into the living room.

"There's the man now!" Harrison swooped up the little boy in a way that twanged some distinctly maternal chords deep within Carrie.

"You remember Carrie, don't you?" Harrison brought him over to her.

"Cawee." Nathan pointed.

"Well, Carrie is going to stay with you today while Uncle Harrison goes into the office. I'll be back after your nap."

Nathan looked doubtful and Carrie wasn't sure he understood that Harrison was leaving.

Harrison kept up a gentle patter as he put Nathan into the high chair and gave him a handful of cereal to keep him occupied. Nicely done, Carrie thought. Temporary fatherhood was growing on him.

"Gotta go." He hesitated. "Carrie, I do appreciate you giving up your day off to help me. I...like to think you're the sort of person who'd help me out even if I weren't on the board."

And did Carrie say, "Of course I am"? Did she say "Thanks"? Did she manage a witty reply? No, she stood there with her mouth open, looking like a dead fish while Harrison let himself out.

"Matthew, your uncle is a very complex man," she said, staring at the closed door. "I definitely wrote him off too quickly."

Free! Free, free, free.

Harrison almost felt guilty at the euphoria he experienced driving away from his condo. Almost.

Feeling guilty would require a lot more sleep than he'd had in the past two days. Matthew had been up in the night again and Harrison wondered how long this teething business was going to last.

As he pulled into his parking space, he thought about Carrie and how he owed her for today.

Yes, he'd agreed to talk with the board, but he wondered why she'd let herself accumulate ten violations. Minor violations, true, but why give the board an excuse? If remaining at White Oak Bayou was so important to her, then why did she go out of her way to violate the policies?

She also had a point about being singled out.

Harrison had felt uncomfortable about citing her for the recycling bin, but he'd been outvoted.

Yes, Carrie Brent was a difficult woman to figure out, not that he'd tried very hard. He felt the constant quibbling between her and the board was a time waster and he avoided people who wasted time. But she hadn't wasted time this weekend—at least not his. Maybe he should try harder to figure her out.

This morning, she'd looked appealingly domestic, with her hair in a ponytail and wearing shorts and a T-shirt. Another Carrie incarnation, he supposed, as he walked into his office. He actually found himself looking forward to her next one.

In spite of leaving his home later than he'd intended, Harrison still arrived before Sharon, his assistant.

Good. This would give him enough time to check Jon's calendar and see what he needed to cover.

Harrison left his briefcase by his desk and walked through the connecting door into Jon's office.

On the desk, was a framed picture of Matthew and Nathan and the Easter Bunny. Harrison had seen the picture before, but now, knowing the boys better, he took the time to study it. Matthew had grown in the past couple of months. Nathan's curls were longer. It was time to get that boy a haircut, Harrison thought, putting the picture back on Jon's desk.

Harrison scanned Jon's calendar and memo pad. Nothing out of the ordinary.

The message light on the phone was blinking. Normally Harrison wouldn't listen to private messages, but since Jon was going to be gone the entire week and Stephanie was away from home as well, he retrieved the voice mail.

There were three messages. The first two were acknowledgments from people Jon had rescheduled. Good.

It was the third message that made Harrison's blood run cold.

"Jon, great news!" Felicia's voice sounded in his ear. "I don't know what you said to him, but Harrison agreed to the domestic time-management book. We need to move on this. I was able to clear my schedule, so I can hop down there to Houston with the contract and we can brainstorm. Monday is good for me, so if I don't hear from you, I'll plan on seeing you say, lunchtime?"

Oh, great. He had only one guaranteed workday without the kids, and he didn't want to waste it on an unscheduled visit from his publisher.

Harrison raced back to his office and called Felicia, hoping to catch her before she left.

He got her voice mail. He didn't leave a message.

If she expected to be here for lunch, then she was already headed to the airport.

"What does she think she's doing dropping in like this? Didn't she read my book?" Exhaling heavily, Harrison sank into his leather chair and swiveled it to face the office windows.

Rothwell's Rules dealt with people like Felicia. One strategy was to tell them firmly, but politely, to make an appointment, then refuse to see them.

Harrison acknowledged that the tactic only worked when dealing with subordinates or peers. Felicia, in charge of his book, was neither. Felicia was someone he couldn't afford to tick off, so even though she was expecting to meet with Jon, Harrison would have to see her.

Though he didn't consider himself a typical author, he knew that *Rothwell's Rules* was responsible for bringing in much of his company's business as well as being the syllabus on which his highly lucrative seminars were based.

But without introducing something new, even though Harrison felt his work stood as it was, his success would become stale. Cosmetic updates would eventually be recognized for what they were.

It was time, so to speak, for something new and the *Domestic Primer* was the way to go. Felicia was enthusiastic enough about the idea to fly to Houston and Harrison wanted her enthusiastic. Therefore, inconvenient as it was, he would meet with her.

It was the entertaining part that bothered him. Felicia would expect him to take her to lunch as well as dinner.

What would he do with the boys? Carrie couldn't baby-sit because she had to work.

What was he going to do with the boys?

The thought resonated through his mind enough times during the day, that Harrison began looking with suspicion upon each employee who had children. Were they concentrating on their jobs, or were they worrying about their children?

How much time was wasted due to preoccupation with family?

And, incidentally, just how was Carrie getting along with his nephews?

Harrison closed the door to his office and guiltily punched his home number.

There was no answer. How could there be no answer? Where were they? As possibilities—all of them bad—occurred to him, he left a distracted message to himself and hoped Carrie would listen to it.

Trying to concentrate, he dealt with a number of minor tasks, rescheduled meetings and cleared the afternoon for Felicia.

Then he called Carrie again. "Where were you?" he demanded as soon as she answered the telephone.

"I took the boys outside for a walk," she answered calmly.

Oh. "That wasn't on the schedule." He was being ridiculous.

"I know."

"Carrie, you *are* following the schedule, aren't you?"

"More ravioli, Nathan?"

"Carrie—"

"I'm attempting to follow a schedule of sorts."

"I want you to follow *my* schedule."

He heard paper crackling. "Hmm. Argue with Harrison...nope, not on the schedule. Goodbye, Harry."

She hung up. Harrison redialed immediately.

"Don't worry, I'm taking notes," she said as soon as she picked up the phone.

"I'm sorry. I was...worried that something bad had happened when I couldn't reach you earlier." He mumbled the last.

There was silence. He hoped he wouldn't have to repeat his apology.

She sighed. "You know, it's a lot easier not to like you when you're being a jerk. You aren't being a very good jerk, Harry."

Why didn't she want to like him? "Sorry. I know I can do better."

They both laughed. "Say, is Carrie your given name, or is it short for something?"

"Uh..." He heard a clatter. "Nathan just dumped his bowl on the floor. Gotta go!"

So, she could dish it out, but she couldn't take it. Harrison was laughing when he hung up the phone. Just for that, he was going to call the condo management office and find out what name was on Carrie's lease.

And then he'd use it.

He'd looked up the number when a female voice sang out, "Knock, knock?" The connecting door between his office and Jon's opened and Felicia stuck her head in. "I heard laughing. Does that mean you're in a good mood, I hope?"

"Relatively." Harrison replaced the telephone without completing his call. "How are you, Felicia?"

She took that as an invitation to enter. "Was my face red when your secretary told me Jon was away this week. She said I could use his office to make a few quick calls, by the way."

Harrison nodded, watching as the dark-haired, dark-eyed Felicia approached his desk.

Carrie had dark hair and dark eyes, but the two women were completely different. Carrie was, well Carrie. Felicia was taller, thinner and looked a lot more New Yorky.

And both of them ignored his schedules.

"I suppose Jon told you about my visit."

Harrison shook his head. "Did he know you planned to come to Houston?"

Felicia laughed without a hint of apology. "Perhaps not." She carefully folded herself into a chair and crossed her legs. "So I'll just have to talk with you."

No apology. No acknowledgment that she'd shot his day to pieces. "If I'd known in advance that you wanted to meet with me, then I could have cleared a larger chunk of time in my schedule." But he'd cleared time, hadn't he? She'd known he would. Felicia was getting what she wanted.

"You and your schedules. But I shouldn't complain. They've made us both a potful of money, haven't they?" She tilted her head and gave him an amused smile.

"That, they have." Felicia was a striking woman, as well as being supremely intelligent, Harrison thought dispassionately. If there ever could be anything between them, he might have pursued her, but the distance involved made a relationship too much of an effort.

"I brought your contract with me," she said. "Sharon has sent it on to your legal department."

"Since you could have faxed it or sent it by courier, I'm assuming there is another reason for your visit?" He chose not to tell her he'd listened to Jon's voice mail.

Too, he was annoyed by the way she'd circumvented Sharon. What if he'd been talking with a client?

"Yes. I wanted to kick around a few ideas with Jon and see if we could coordinate efforts and get the most advertising bang for our buck. I also wanted to see how he planned to handle your weak spot."

Harrison bristled. "What weak spot?"

Felicia laughed, gesturing grandly. "Harrison, you've never been married! You have no children. Now, *I* realize you can organize the world, but our target market is parents—specifically mothers. They don't appreciate being told how to live their lives from someone who hasn't walked the walk. As soon as we announce your book on domestic time management, critics will pounce."

"I am 'walking the walk' even as we speak," Harrison was pleased to tell her. "Jon's kids are staying with me for the week."

"Fabulous! How old are they?"

"Nathan will be two in October and Matthew is about seven months old."

"Oh, my." Felicia inclined her head. "I am impressed." Eyebrows raised, she made a show of looking around the room. "And where are your nephews now?"

"At home with the sitter. I spent all weekend alone with them." Mostly alone. For all practical purposes alone. "Matthew is teething," he added for emphasis.

"Good."

"I already have ideas for chapters."

"Even better. How about taking me to lunch and we can discuss them?"

Lunch with Felicia dragged on. Harrison's state of mind wasn't helped by knowing he'd been outmaneuvered. By remaining at the restaurant, Felicia had a captive audience and no office interruptions. She was the perfect example of the exception to *Rothwell's Rules*.

As two-thirty approached, Harrison ended their lunch. "As productive as our lunch has been—" which was true "—I've been out of reach for a couple of hours and I'm nervous about leaving my nephews with a new sitter. I should be checking in."

"Just like a real parent!" Felicia rose gracefully.

"Now *this* sort of anecdotal information will give your book that added verisimilitude."

Whatever. Harrison's only concern was wresting control of his day back from Felicia.

When they got back to the office, Harrison headed straight for Sharon.

"Yes, there have been plenty of messages," she said, glancing pointedly at Felicia.

Felicia smiled blankly.

Sharon listed the calls as she handed the message slips to Harrison. "...and fourteen calls from Carrie Brent."

Adrenaline shot through Harrison's system. The kids. "What's happened?" *Why* had he come into work today? Why had he trusted Carrie Brent, of all people, with his nephews? What did he really know about her?

"I told her you were at lunch," an aggrieved Sharon continued. "I *refused* to tell her where, and for this—"

"*What's happened?*" Harrison snarled at her.

Sharon stuttered in surprise. "I—I don't know. She wouldn't tell me until I told her where you were, and *I* wouldn't—"

"She's watching the boys today! Something must have happened." Harrison hurried into his office and grabbed for the telephone.

With each ring, his anxiety increased. "Where *is* she?"

He slammed the telephone back into the cradle and stared at it, trying to figure out what to do next.

"Sharon says that your baby-sitter apparently has a conflict and wanted to speak to you about it,"

Felicia said soothingly. She approached the desk and leaned against it.

"The kids are okay?"

"She didn't say that they weren't."

Harrison exhaled and Felicia laughed. "Oh, I like this side of you, Harrison. Very paternal. Very strong, caring male." She lowered her voice. "Very attractive."

Harrison didn't feel attractive. "I will strangle her. Where could she be?"

Reaching for the phone again, he stopped at the sound of a high-pitched voice. "Hawee!"'

Whipping around, he watched Nathan's chubby legs churn up the carpet as he gleefully ran the length of the hall from the elevators to Harrison's office. Behind him, Carrie wheeled Matthew in his stroller.

Felicia made a strangled sound. "*That,* I take it, is the baby-sitter?"

CHAPTER FIVE

HARRISON was so relieved to see everyone in one piece that all he could do was swing Nathan up in his arms and watch Carrie's progress.

She wore a real short denim skirt, flat shoes and a tight sweater that showed her stomach when she moved her arms. Her hair was all over the place.

She looked great, until he realized that she no longer looked domestic and that undoubtedly meant bad news for him.

"I've been trying to call you," she announced as she wheeled Matthew's stroller through the doorway. Behind her, she'd left wheel marks in the hall carpet all the way to the elevator.

Harrison indicated the stack of messages. "So I've been told. I just returned from lunch."

"You did?" Carrie looked down at her watch. "Wow."

Harrison cleared his throat. "This is Felicia LaCrosse, my publisher. She flew in from New York this morning." Not that it was any of Carrie's business. "Felicia, this is Carrie Brent, the neighbor who's baby-sitting for me."

Felicia raised an eyebrow, but politely acknowledged Carrie. "And these must be Jon's children."

"Yes, this is Nathan, and that's Matthew in the stroller." Harrison turned so the little boy in his arms faced Felicia.

Felicia smiled at Nathan, who promptly stuck his

finger into his mouth and leaned his head on Harrison's shoulder.

"He's still sleepy," Carrie said. "I had to wake him up from his nap."

Why? Harrison wanted to know.

Felicia knelt and made gooey noises at Matthew in the stroller.

Over her head, he frowned at Carrie. "I thought we agreed five o'clock." He kept his voice calm, considering Carrie had just put him through several tense minutes and now had appeared, children in tow, at his office.

This made two workdays in a row that Harrison's personal life had impinged on his professional one. The very tenets of his corporate philosophy were at risk and he didn't like it.

Though technically he could defend himself by saying that the children *were* business, since he was using them as research, he had a feeling his employees would point out that it was still an interruption.

Carrie's face was the picture of remorse. "We did say five, and I'm sorry, but I completely forgot about the interview I'd set up for this afternoon."

"You forgot an interview?"

"Well, I left a note on my refrigerator, but since I wasn't at home, I didn't see it."

Which was why she should have a personal agenda, Harrison thought. His company made an excellent one.

"Anyway," Carrie continued, "this group has a fabulous buzz and they're headed east after tomorrow night." She was speaking very fast and gesturing with both hands. "They're rehearsing this afternoon and Gabe—he's the club owner and he's liked me ever since I gave Izzy's a good write-up—well, Gabe said they'd talk to me and no one else today. Can you believe it?'' Carrie's enthusiasm was long-winded, but contagious. ''I'll have my review in before anyone else hears them!''

She finished with a wide smile as though Harrison should be thrilled for her and not as though she'd just wrecked what few hours remained of his workday.

Felicia stood. ''You know, discovering new talent is a hobby of mine. What's the name of the group?''

''The Bayou Buzzards. Isn't that rank?''

''Well, obviously, that'll have to change. Are they coming to New York?''

As Harrison stood there, ignored in his own office, Carrie and Felicia carried on their conversation. Why hadn't he ever heard about this ''hobby'' of Felicia's before?

Nathan's eyes drooped shut and he drooled on Harrison's sixty-dollar silk tie. ''I presume this means you propose to leave the children with me?'' he inquired.

Both Carrie and Felicia stared at him.

''Well, of course she's leaving the children with you,'' Felicia said. ''She's got a great opportunity for a scoop.''

They were ganging up on him, these schedule smashers. ''You realize this means that we won't be able to go over the contract with the lawyers this afternoon and as for tonight...'' Harrison gestured toward the children.

Nathan was asleep, and Matthew was beginning to fuss. Carrie dug a bottle out of the diaper bag.

''Oh, let me!'' Felicia knelt by the stroller and held the bottle. ''These things happen in real life, Harrison.

In fact, this is a good experience for you. Pretend Carrie is your wife and you've got to coordinate schedules with her. That's the way real parents operate.''

"I have *never* witnessed a wife dumping the children at her husband's office.''

"That's because the husbands have dumped them first,'' Carrie muttered.

Felicia laughed.

Harrison did not.

"I don't mind about tonight,'' Felicia said. "I'd like to see you interact with the kids. Now, are we ordering in, or cooking?''

If Felicia saw his home in its current state, she'd think her organizational guru had gone amok. She'd reconsider the whole domestic organization project. Harrison wasn't ready for Felicia—or anyone—to see him "interacting" with his nephews.

How can I get out of this? Harrison sent a look of pure desperation toward Carrie, but what could she do except cause more trouble?

"I've seen Harrison interact with the kids. It's no big thrill,'' she said.

"Gee, thanks.''

"You know what I mean, Harry. But listen, Felicia, why don't you come with me and check out the Bayou Buzzards?''

Felicia's face lit up. "*Could* I?''

"Sure! Maybe we can help them think of a new name.''

Carrie and Felicia? Together? This wasn't a good idea.

But he didn't have a better one.

Abandoning Matthew and the bottle, Felicia

grabbed her purse and ran toward Jon's office. "Let me make a quick call and I'll be right with you!"

He had to stop this. "Felicia, wait a minute—"

"I left the car seat with your guard downstairs," Carrie informed him.

"She can't go with you," Harrison said.

"Why not?" Carrie dug into her purse, pulled out a mirror and checked her appearance, then replaced the mirror and looked at him, an expectant expression on her face.

"Because she's my publisher." *Because I want her to remain my publisher.*

"I know." Carrie lifted Matthew out of the stroller. "You can thank me later, say, Thursday night at the board meeting?"

"*Thank* you?"

"Yeah." Carrie grinned. "For baby-sitting *her* tonight."

Glancing toward the open door to Jon's office, Harrison leaned forward and lowered his voice, "Carrie, don't blow this for me."

She matched his tone. "I am pulling your chestnuts out of the fire and you know it. If she watched you try to follow that stupid schedule you gave me, she'd realize you don't have a clue about living with children."

"I—"

"Don't worry, I left you a modified schedule. Besides, your place is kind of messy. I didn't have a chance to finish my laundry. Just push it out of the way."

Harrison clamped his eyes shut as he envisioned his living room draped with toys and laundry and assorted Carrie debris.

"I'll come back for my clothes later tonight."

Harrison hoped her voice hadn't carried through the open door of his office. Sharon must be getting an earful.

Propping Matthew on one hip, Carrie shoved Harrison's telephone, calendar and the rain forest waterfall tube someone had given him off to one side. "You can lay Nathan there while you finish feeding Matthew."

Naturally Nathan woke up the minute Harrison put him on the desk. Carrie handed Matthew to Harrison and gave Nathan a bag of raisins and the rain forest tube.

Harrison started to object, but Nathan was transfixed by the whooshing sound the tube made, so Harrison mentally wrote off the tube. "Hello, Matthew, you want the rest of this bottle?"

Matthew regarded him owlishly, then burped up a significant portion of the bottle he'd just been fed.

"I guess I should have given you a burp cloth," Carrie said. Belatedly she handed him one.

Harrison mopped up himself and cranky Matthew.

He was shrugging out of his jacket when Felicia came back into the room. "I hope I wasn't too long."

"No, but we've got to hustle." Carrie waved bye-bye to Nathan.

"Harrison, I'll see you tomorrow," Felicia said.

He looked up. "I thought you were going back to New York tomorrow."

"You haven't signed the contract yet."

At this point, Harrison would consider signing just about anything. Instead he smiled and murmured something, which was drowned out by Matthew coughing and spitting up on Harrison's shirt.

"You might want to hold his head a little higher when you're feeding him so he won't swallow so much air," Carrie said, and then they left.

Harrison promptly closed the door after them. "Now she tells me," he muttered as he loosened his tie and dropped it onto the desk.

Fortunately, because he was an organized person in another life, Harrison kept spare shirts in his office. One-handed, he yanked off the shirt. Matthew looked as if he was about to cry, so Harrison tried patting his back.

How had he, Harrison Rothwell, arguably the most organized man in Texas, maybe the world, ended up feeding an infant with digestive problems in his office?

"Hawee?"

"Yes, Nathan?"

"Joose?"

The bag of raisins was empty. Harrison suspected that some of them had been poked into holes in the rain forest tube. Could Carrie have possibly packed juice in the diaper bag?

He started looking through it when his office door burst open and Carrie ran back in. "I left my car keys in the diaper bag!" She came to a complete halt when she saw Harrison. She stared at him, an arrested expression on her face.

"I was looking for juice," he said.

"Cawee!"

At the sound of Nathan's voice, Carrie seemed to remember where she was. "Did you want juice, Nathan?"

"Joose!" He tried to climb off the desk. Harrison

hurried over and picked him up, then turned to face Carrie, a baby in each arm.

She visibly swallowed. "You—you…are you going to go through the rest of the day dressed like that? Or not dressed like that?"

"No," Harrison answered, amused for probably the first time today. And, to be honest, a little flattered. "I have spare shirts here in the office."

"That's, uh, good." Still she stood there.

"Carrie?"

"Mmm?"

"The juice?"

"Right…the juice." She opened the tiny bottle, poured it into Nathan's cup and snapped on the lid.

Harrison set him back on the desk and pushed a chair next to it, so Nathan could climb down on his own if he wanted.

Carrie handed him the cup, then stuck her hands into the pockets of her skirt and watched the little boy drink in between glances at Harrison.

"Carrie? Your car keys? You're in a hurry? You've abandoned my publisher who knows where?"

Her eyes widened. "Oh!" She retrieved her keys, then pointed. "Nathan is chewing on your tie." She turned and ran back to the elevator.

Harrison watched her run.

Her skirt was very short. He liked that in a skirt.

He caught Sharon staring at him, and closed his door.

Curiously he wasn't angry, though he felt he had every right to be. He wasn't even embarrassed, or frazzled, nor did he feel out of control.

Numb, that's what he was.

Matthew was falling asleep, so Harrison gently laid him in the stroller.

Picking a shirt out of his drawer, he looked down at the ruins of his tie. "Nathan, you've got great taste."

After Carrie's warning, Harrison expected the worst when he arrived home.

He wasn't in the best of moods, his curious numbness having worn off by the third time Sharon had laughed at him this afternoon.

Even allowing for the familiarity that working together since the beginning of the company had given them, Sharon was enjoying his travails more than she should have.

The female traffic at her desk had increased, too, and every time he'd opened his office door, he'd faced a crowd around Sharon's desk.

When he'd finally packed it in for the day, and had put both boys in the stroller and wheeled them down the hall, it was to the sound of applause.

So, no, he wasn't thrilled that Carrie had put him in the position of trying to eke out a few minutes of work while keeping Nathan and Matthew from destroying his office, but then it wasn't her problem.

It was his.

Harrison had also spent too much time figuring out how to strap Matthew's infant carrier and the bulky toddler car seat into his car.

He was beginning to realize that children took up more time and effort than he'd ever dreamed.

But that didn't mean there couldn't be schedules. Granted, there had to be concessions. For instance, he needed to take his suit jacket to the dry cleaners, and ordinarily would have stopped on his way home, but it wasn't worth unloading the boys from the car this time. He'd never have thought of it if he hadn't actually had the experience with his nephews.

Arriving at his door at last, Harrison hesitated before unlocking it. Drawing a deep breath, he opened the door.

He noticed the laundry right away, but surprisingly, that was the only jarring note. Everything else was put away. Even the kitchen was clean. Harrison was impressed.

Nathan walked past him directly to a box that contained toys and dug around in it. Harrison dragged in the stroller and set Matthew in the playpen. Carrie's laptop was still on the coffee table. With an eye on Nathan, Harrison moved the computer to high ground.

He found his schedule on the bar. Beside it was a new one written by Carrie. After scanning the part of the day that had already passed, Harrison skipped down to dinnertime.

Carrie had suggested letting the boys play together while the meal was assembled. If they were restless, she listed alternatives.

It all looked so easy, but Harrison knew better. Okay, he'd follow her schedule and when everything fell apart, then he'd let her know.

But nothing fell apart and at nine-thirty, Harrison found himself sitting on his couch, trying to ignore the interesting pile of Carrie's underwear, while contemplating his whole life's philosophy.

Naturally this was the moment Carrie chose to knock quietly on his door.

Silently he opened it.

She peeked around him to see the sleeping

Matthew, then whispered. "You followed the schedule, I see." Without asking, she walked in.

"How do you know?"

"Because it's nine-thirty, everything's done and this is the 'parent' time." She patted the sofa. "Go ahead and sit back down. I'll just get my underwear out of the way."

Harrison chose not to argue, mainly because he couldn't think of any reason to. "And what is supposed to happen during parent time?" He watched as she handled underwear ranging from plain cotton to leopard silk.

"Recharging. Reconnecting. Talking. Drinking decaf." She grinned. "Working on brothers and sisters for the kids."

"Folding underwear?"

"Normally not, I think."

Harrison managed a smile. "You'll notice that I haven't asked about Felicia. That doesn't mean that I don't want to know about your evening together, but it does mean that I don't want to hear bad news."

Carrie made a face at him. "She had a great time. The group is fabulous and she gave them her card."

"Why?"

"She wants to see that they meet the right people in New York. That woman has more connections than a spider."

It was a vividly accurate portrayal of Felicia.

"I can see why you were worried about antagonizing her," Carrie added, stuffing the last of her underwear into a pillowcase.

"I wasn't worried."

"Oh, *Harry,* I saw that look of panic on your face."

"That wasn't panic, that was justifiable concern."

Carrie gave him a look and headed for the kitchen. "Did you put my stuff in the dryer?"

Did he— "No!"

"Don't shout. You'll wake up Matthew."

Several minutes later, Harrison heard the dryer start. Carrie returned to the room, sat on the sofa next to him and curled her legs beneath her. "We talked about you."

Instantly a knot formed in his stomach.

"She kind of has a thing for you."

"I don't want to know this."

"Why not? You can use it to manipulate her." Carrie propped her elbow on the back of the sofa and rested her chin on her hand.

Harrison gave her a hard look. "I don't like what you're implying. And...and I don't need to manipulate people that way. My work stands on its own merits."

She raised her eyebrows. "Well, Harry, judging by the schedule you left me, you're going to need help with your next book. A little manipulation on your part wouldn't be amiss."

Next book. He hadn't known Carrie was aware of Rothwell's Rules. Obviously they *had* discussed him. That meant Felicia thought Carrie was a more integral part of his life than she was. Knowing Carrie, she'd encouraged the impression.

"Felicia says your sales have fallen off and you need to come out with something different or your company will go belly up."

Astonishment rendered him mute for several seconds. "My company is doing just fine, thank you," he said stiffly. "Sometimes Felicia forgets that

Rothwell Time Management Consultants spawned the book and not the other way around." The gall of Felicia discussing his private business with Carrie made him wonder just who else she'd discussed him with.

"Don't get so prickly. It was just girl talk."

His life's work was reduced to "girl talk"? "I'm not 'prickly' but I do resent my publisher discussing personal business with a stranger."

Carrie touched her throat. "Me? I'm not a stranger."

"Yes, you are."

"You'd let a stranger watch your nephews?"

Jon's words echoed in his mind. *I'm not leaving them with a stranger for a week.* "No," he admitted reluctantly.

"You see?"

"Nevertheless, I would rather that Felicia had kept her views of my situation to herself."

Carrie leaned forward. "Come on, you can talk to me. We've bonded over laundry and kids."

"We have not bonded. We are not bonding. I don't want to bond."

"Sure you do."

"I do?" Did he? He gazed at the woman sitting in the muted lamplight. Right now, she looked like Mona Lisa with a bad perm.

"Uh-huh." One of Carrie's curls slipped forward and she tucked it behind her ear.

Okay, maybe the perm wasn't so bad.

Actually none of Carrie was bad.

Heart beating faster, Harrison swallowed. "Why do you say that?"

"You've been staring at my legs."

"I have not!" Involuntarily Harrison's gaze flicked to her legs.

Carrie, batting her eyelashes, raised the already short hem of her skirt another inch.

"Stop that!"

"Why? Don't you want to kiss me?"

She'd asked a legitimate question. Why couldn't he answer her?

Maybe he didn't like the answer. Maybe she was right. Maybe he did want to kiss her.

But he wasn't going to. Harrison shifted away from her. "Are you always so direct?"

"Only when the situation calls for it."

"This situation doesn't call for it."

"Glad to hear it." Somehow, she'd lessened the gap between them and was well within reach.

"Carrie…"

"Yes?" Her arm stretched along the back of the sofa until her fingers brushed his shoulder.

He flinched and she smiled.

"Carrie." He took her hand and set it away from him. "You're a very attractive woman—"

"Oh, not the 'you're a very attractive woman, *but*' speech." She rolled her eyes. "I already know the next part."

"Carrie, you don't understand—"

"Yes, I do. Let's see, it's not me, it's you, right?"

"Yes."

"And you don't think *anything*—" She wiggled her hands back and forth "—between us would be appropriate because—and here's where you stretch for an excuse to spare my feelings." She gazed around the room, then hooked a thumb toward the playpen. "Because Matthew is over there sleeping soundly, never mind that he's behind this sofa and we could turn out the light.'' She gave Harrison a look from beneath her lashes. ''Or, we could always adjourn elsewhere.''

His throat tightened. ''Matthew's not the problem.''

''I figured he wasn't. But there is one, isn't there?''

Harrison nodded. ''I'm on the condo board and I don't want anyone's expectations to become greater than they should be.''

She straightened, a look of outrage on her face. ''You think I'm trying to seduce you so you'll influence the board?''

Harrison opened his mouth, then closed it. No matter what he said, she would interpret it negatively. Closing his eyes he let his head fall back onto the sofa pillow. ''I don't want to be accused of using you, especially if the board refuses to dismiss your citation. Having said that, I refuse to think any more tonight.''

''Oh, Harry. We already had a deal for the board—baby-sitting in exchange for an eloquent plea on my behalf. Are you reneging?''

''Of course not.''

''And you aren't going to try to seduce me into helping you with your new book?''

He kept his eyes closed. ''I don't need your help.''

''Yes, you do, but since we're even on the board thing, you'll have to lure me here another way. I'm a busy woman. I work nights. You work days. Kissing me is your only hope if you want to get that book published.''

She was being so absurd that Harrison laughed and opened his eyes. ''You're something else.''

She lifted a shoulder. ''So I've been told.''

Acting with a rare impulse, Harrison reached behind her neck, brought her head to his and kissed her.

He meant to release her quickly and share a laugh about calling her bluff, but Carrie settled against him, her hair curling across his face, bringing with it the bewitching scent he'd come to associate with her.

Harrison took the kiss to a dangerous depth almost instantly—dangerous if he meant to share a laugh and nothing more.

Dangerous if he wanted to stop anytime soon.

But he didn't and he couldn't. Carrie's kiss was bright. Clear. Intense. Vivid.

Potent.

It was as individual as she was, but why had he thought kissing Carrie would be like kissing anyone else? She wasn't like anyone else he'd ever known. It stood to reason that her kiss would be different, as well.

It wasn't the sort of different he thought he'd craved, either. His tastes ran more toward the predictable sophistication of someone like, say Felicia.

He'd actually kissed Felicia once when *Rothwell's Rules* had been selected for some honor he couldn't remember now. But at the time, the occasion had been worthy enough for a quick, impulsive kiss that had lingered just the slightest bit beyond impulsive, though immediately afterward, they'd both pretended not to have noticed.

Kissing Felicia had been pleasant enough, but they would have had to work to develop any more passionate feelings, and they both knew it.

Yet from the moment Carrie's lips had met his, Harrison hadn't had to work at anything. He'd just felt.

And what he'd felt was the passion—right there, simmering between them.

When had that happened?

Who cared?

They were breaking all the rules for a first kiss. A first kiss was one of exploration, and of learning and testing. A first kiss hinted at what might be. A first kiss didn't reveal everything.

A first kiss wasn't supposed to be one of the singular sensual experiences of his life.

Carrie must not know the rules for first kisses.

And Harrison wasn't about to tell her.

He skimmed his hands down her back and idly caressed the soft skin revealed by her sweater, while he concentrated on the feel of her mouth against his.

He had no idea how much time had elapsed when Carrie raised her head and smiled down at him. "Now, that wasn't so bad, was it?"

Mutely he shook his head.

Not bad? For him, time and all conscious thought had ceased and for her it was "not bad"?

He'd show her "not bad." He reached for her again, but Carrie laughed and stood. "You're a good sport, Harrison. That's why we get along so well together."

"A good sport?"

"Yeah. Some people are too full of themselves to take a little teasing. You played right along." She turned.

"W-where are you going?" He was having trouble assembling a coherent sentence.

"The dryer buzzed. My laundry's done." Then, as if they'd been doing nothing more personal than watching television together, she walked through the kitchen.

Harrison stared after her. Good sport? Teasing?

He hadn't heard the dryer buzz. He probably wouldn't have heard the dryer if it had exploded.

She thought their kiss was a joke?

Did that mean *she'd* been joking when she kissed him?

Harrison tried to swallow and found that his mouth had suddenly gone dry. If that hadn't been a real kiss, then what were her real kisses like?

Thankful to whatever kernel of self-preservation had enabled her to walk away from Harrison Rothwell's kiss, Carrie managed to get all the way through the kitchen before her knees gave out. She clutched the dryer, its warmth equal to the heat in her cheeks. "Oh, man, am I in trouble now."

CHAPTER SIX

ON TUESDAYS and Thursdays, Nathan and Matthew attended a nursery school play group until two o'clock in the afternoon. Harrison planned to take full advantage of the boys' absence. He also planned to leave the office at two o'clock, take the boys home and stay there.

He would not ask Carrie to baby-sit. She was dangerous to his peace of mind. She had to work tonight, anyway. And before he saw her again, he had to organize his jumbled thoughts concerning her.

His thoughts had no business being jumbled, no matter what sort of kiss they'd shared. It had been a casual kiss. A good one, yes, but a one-time thing. Carrie had called him a good sport and so he would be. He should be grateful she wasn't the type who would try to parlay the kiss into something it shouldn't be.

It had been an impulsive kiss with a little more chemistry than he'd expected, that was all. He'd forget about it.

By now Carrie surely had.

To give her credit, he'd followed her schedule this morning and everything had gone like clockwork. The trick seemed to be to do more than one minor task at a time and being able to interrupt one, start another, then return to the first one when the opportunity arose.

It would be a new way of implementing *Rothwell's*

89

Rules, but Harrison had never shied away from a challenge.

He'd have to remember to thank Carrie when he saw her again, which wouldn't be anytime soon.

"I put Ms. LaCrosse and Clifton from legal in your office," Sharon informed him when he passed by her desk at 9:27.

"Thanks, Sharon." Harrison picked up the pile of messages and memos that he normally would have dealt with by this time of the morning, and walked into his office.

"Hello, Harrison." Felicia glanced at her watch. "Just in time. I've got a noon flight."

"Let's get started, then." He took the contract and reviewed the pages with tape flags on them while Felicia talked.

She was full of praise for Carrie and kept referring to her as Harrison's assistant. "I understand that you're taking advantage of an unexpected opportunity because both Jon and his wife are away, so I was very impressed when Carrie told me all you've done."

What had Carrie told her?

Fortunately Felicia went on to explain. As Harrison listened, it became apparent that Carrie had done a full-scale PR push worthy of any professional. He smiled to himself. Public relations must have been another one of Carrie's past professions. Too bad she didn't realize that Felicia was a grand master at PR, herself.

"It's obvious that you know what you're doing," Felicia said after they'd both signed the contract. The lawyer had left, and she was preparing to leave for the airport. "But I'm telling you, it still would be better from a marketing standpoint if you were married with a family of your own." She smiled. "Think about it. You have plenty of time before the book comes out."

Trust Felicia to reduce the momentous decision to marry and raise children to a marketing opportunity.

"At any rate, I'm going to enjoy working with Carrie on this project."

Carrie? Wait a minute. "Working with Carrie?"

"Yes, on the nitty-gritty parts. I do realize you have a company to run, Harrison, so I don't expect to monopolize your time. Having a research assistant is an excellent idea. I'm glad I had a chance to meet her." Felicia smiled. "This is going to work."

Now was not the time to argue about Carrie's role, or lack of one. "Certainly, it is," Harrison said, and opened the door.

Felicia laughed. "I'll confess that I had my doubts about you being able to pull off this project when Jon first called."

Harrison's grip on the side of the door tightened, but Felicia didn't notice.

"He wasn't happy that we were planning to remainder *Rothwell's Rules,* but the company is trimming its publishing list and warehouse space is expensive." She gestured with her sunglasses. "What could I do?"

This was all news to Harrison, but he wasn't about to admit it.

"Unless you came up with some brilliant change, there wasn't any point in going back for another printing, was there?" Felicia continued.

Let *Rothwell's Rules* go out of print? The implication was that his time-management system was a passing fad. Harrison could already predict the effect the news would have on potential customers.

"But Jon mentioned that you were considering expanding into the domestic arena. To tell you the truth, I was skeptical at first. *Rothwell's Rules* is more idealistic than practical—I could only imagine what you'd come up with for poor frazzled parents."

More idealistic than practical? "A dozen Fortune 500 companies have found it practical enough to implement," he said pointedly.

"I know your stats. That's why I listened to Jon. He persuaded me to take a chance on your new project, but I needed to get marketing behind the proposal. That's why I flew down here. And I must say, I'm extremely glad I did. Carrie is a gem, Harrison. With her ideas and your organizational skills, I think we've got another winner."

Harrison was stunned, though he attempted not to show it. He murmured who-knew-what to Felicia, said goodbye, then closed his door.

Felicia thought Carrie was his assistant. Felicia thought Harrison couldn't formulate a domestic time-management system on his own. Felicia thought Carrie's ideas—whatever they might be—were good.

Just how had Carrie insinuated herself into his life?

Harrison sat in his desk chair, swiveled it to face the windows and contemplated the fact that the biggest project he'd undertaken since forming Rothwell Management Consultants apparently hinged on the participation of his unpredictable neighbor.

And he didn't like it.

Carrie wasn't his assistant. She'd only baby-sat for part of a day, for pity's sake.

Now what was he going to do?

* * *

Harrison was going to demonstrate that he didn't need Carrie's help, that's what he was going to do.

He arrived early at the nursery school and spoke with the boys' teachers and gave his card to as many parents as he could and collected the telephone numbers of those who would agree to complete the survey he'd decided to take.

He also observed the patient teachers interact with various age groups of children.

All in all, it was a productive hour and when he arrived home with the boys, he immediately wanted to write up his notes. Matthew and Nathan cooperated by both taking naps.

Surely it was a sign that he was on the right track. All right, Harrison thought. What information did he have here?

In suggesting strategies for household management, he'd obviously have to consider single parents, households in which only one parent was employed and households with double-income parents all separately, but there would be elements in common with all three. That's what he intended to develop.

He drafted ideas until the boys woke up.

Now this was the way it was supposed to work, he thought. And tomorrow, he'd test his ideas.

He didn't need Carrie's help at all.

But it looked as if she needed his. Once the boys were asleep, Harrison opened his mail. There, right on the agenda for Thursday's meeting of the White Oak Bayou Condominiums Residents' Board, was an item to discuss initiating eviction proceedings against Carrie Brent.

Ridiculous. She was living in a piece of leftover space. What could they want it for?

He was going to have to be at his most persuasive on Thursday night or she'd be out on her ear.

Harrison tried to think of a line of reasoning he could use, but was too tired. The best thing he could do for her now was get an entire night's sleep.

He'd just drifted off to sleep when he heard Matthew crying. He hadn't finished his bedtime bottle earlier and had been restless during the evening.

Groaning, Harrison climbed out of bed. Frankly he was becoming impatient with the whole teething process. Why couldn't teeth all come in at once and get this misery over with instead of dragging the entire business out for endless days?

There wasn't enough formula left in the can in the refrigerator to fill a bottle, so he went to get another can. Matthew had already gone through an entire case. Jon had only left two cases, but with these extra feedings at night, Harrison was using the stuff up too fast. He pulled the empty box out of the pantry and jerked open the top of the box beneath it.

It had already been opened and offered no resistance, so Harrison banged his elbow on the wall. Muttering, he swiped the flap out of the way. But instead of the case of formula he'd thought it was, he found the box packed with toddler food and snacks for Nathan, along with assorted extra bibs, bottles and rubbery things.

He was out of formula.

Taking what he had into Matthew, Harrison sat on the couch and offered the bottle to him.

Great. Fabulous. How could he have run out of formula?

He hadn't inventoried his supplies, that's how.

True, he'd thought he had two cases of formula, but he should have looked.

Another Rothwell rule broken.

Although he hated to, he was going to call Carrie. Maybe she was home already. Picking up Matthew, he carried him and the bottle into the kitchen where he looked up Carrie's phone number.

He got her answering machine. "This is Carrie. You know the drill." He didn't leave a message.

Drawing a deep breath, he replaced the telephone and resigned himself to loading the children into the car and finding an all-night grocery store.

A different sort of person shopped the stores at two a.m. The quiet of the night seeped into the bright fluorescent-lit aisles as a few people silently went about their business.

Silent, that is, unless, they were accompanied by a cranky toddler and a teething baby. Matthew had finished his bottle, but still cried. Nathan, awakened from a sound sleep, also cried when Harrison wouldn't let him climb out of the basket.

"Out!" Nathan shrieked, loud enough to echo.

The clerk manning the courtesy counter watched him closely. *He probably thinks I've kidnapped these kids,* Harrison thought and tried to act as though he shopped like this all the time.

Both children wailed as he prowled the aisles looking for the baby food section. Checkers stared at him. Shoppers glared at him.

"Those babies should be home in bed," a woman chastised him.

"I'm just baby-sitting," Harrison said, pulling his cart to one side so she could pass. "And I ran out of formula."

She looked skeptical in the kind of way that said she was seconds away from calling Children's Protective Services.

"I swear, I'm just baby-sitting!" he called after her. "They're my nephews."

"Joose!" said Nathan and made a grab for the tiny bottles lining the shelves. He snagged one, but knocked two others to the floor where they shattered, splashing Harrison's feet with glass and juice.

"Nathan, no!" Harrison took the bottle away from him, which made him cry even louder, so he opened it and gave it back to him.

He stared at the mess, which was between him and the formula. What was the protocol here? He looked up and down the aisle, but no one was in sight. With glass crunching under the wheels of the cart, Harrison moved to the end of the aisle just as an announcement boomed over the loud speakers.

"Cleanup on aisle nine."

Nathan dropped the juice bottle. It upended and spilled through the wire basket. "Joose!" he shrieked.

Harrison sighed. "Good shot, kid. That was the only clean section of aisle nine."

Nathan howled.

Matthew cried in long, pitiful whimpers.

Harrison felt like joining them.

"Harrison?"

Oh, terrific. Which of his friends was here to witness this incompetence? He turned his head.

Carrie was wheeling a shopping cart toward him. This time, she wore black jeans, a T-shirt that advertised Izzy's on Richmond, thick eyeliner, dark lipstick and blue fingernail polish.

PLAY "LUCKY 7" AND GET
THREE FREE GIFTS!

HOW TO PLAY:

1. With a coin, carefully scratch off the silver box at the right. Then check the claim chart to see what we have for you — **FREE BOOKS** and a gift — **ALL YOURS! ALL FREE!**

2. Send back this card and you'll receive brand-new Harlequin Romance® novels. These books have a cover price of $3.50 each, but they are yours to keep absolutely free.

3. There's no catch. You're under no obligation to buy anything. We charge nothing —  ZERO — for your first shipment And you don't have to make any minimum number of purchases — not even one!

4. The fact is thousands of readers enjoy receiving books by mail from the Harlequin Reader Service® months before they're available in stores. They like the convenience of home delivery and they love our discount prices!

5. We hope that after receiving your free books you'll want to remain a subscriber. But the choice is yours — to continue or cancel, any time at all! So why not take us up on ou invitation, with no risk of any kind. You'll be glad you did!

YOURS FREE!

PLAY LUCKY 7 FOR THIS EXCITING FREE GIFT!

THIS SURPRISE MYSTERY GIFT COULD BE YOURS FREE WHEN YOU PLAY

LUCKY 7!

NO COST! NO OBLIGATION TO BUY!
NO PURCHASE NECESSARY!

PLAY THE

7 LUCKY SLOT MACHINE GAME!

Just scratch off the silver box with a coin. Then check below to see the gifts you get!

YES!

I have scratched off the silver box. Please send me all the gifts for which I qualify. I understand I am under no obligation to purchase any books, as explained on the back and on the opposite page.

116 HDL CGUN
(U-H-R-07/98)

Name
_____
PLEASE PRINT CLEARLY

Address _____ Apt.#_____

City _____ State _____ Zip _____

7	7	7	**WORTH TWO FREE BOOKS PLUS A BONUS MYSTERY GIFT!**
🍒	🍒	🍒	**WORTH TWO FREE BOOKS!**
♣	♣	♣	**WORTH ONE FREE BOOK!**
🔔	🔔	🍒	**TRY AGAIN!**

Offer limited to one per household and not valid to current Harlequin Romance® subscribers. All orders subject to approval.

The Harlequin Reader Service® — Here's how it works

Accepting free books places you under no obligation to buy anything. You may keep the books and gift and return the shipping statement marked "cancel." If you do not cancel, about a month later we'll send you 6 additional novels, and bill you just $2.90 each, plus 25¢ delivery per book and applicable sales tax, if any.* That's the complete price — and compared to cover prices of $3.50 each — quite a bargain! You may cancel at any time, but if you choose to continue, every month we'll send you 6 more books, which you may either purchase at the discount price...or return to us and cancel your subscription.

*Terms and prices subject to change without notice. Sales tax applicable in N.Y.

BUSINESS REPLY MAIL

FIRST-CLASS MAIL   PERMIT NO. 717   BUFFALO, NY

POSTAGE WILL BE PAID BY ADDRESSEE

HARLEQUIN READER SERVICE
3010 WALDEN AVE
PO BOX 1867
BUFFALO NY 14240-9952

NO POSTAGE
NECESSARY
IF MAILED
IN THE
UNITED STATES

She was an angel. At the sight of her, the tension left Harrison's body. Some of the tension.

"What are you doing?" she asked.

"Traumatizing my nephews."

She grinned. "You look pretty traumatized yourself."

"I ran out of formula," he explained.

"Poor Harry." Turning to Nathan, she picked him up out of the cart, ignoring his juicy hands and clothes and holding him to her. "What's the matter, Nathan?"

He babbled something unintelligible to Harrison, but Carrie must have understood. She picked her way down aisle nine and grabbed a bottle of juice.

Harrison rolled the cart back and forth in an attempt to calm Matthew. Carrie and Nathan were standing in front of a display of assorted baby junk. Nathan pointed and Carrie pulled something off a hook. When she got back to the cart, Harrison saw that it was a cup like the one Nathan used.

She set the little boy back in the cart. "Hang on, Nathan. Let me try to open this without tearing the price code." She did, and within seconds, she'd filled the cup with juice and Nathan was happily—and silently—drinking.

"Thanks," Harrison said when he should have been on the floor kissing her feet. He probably would have, except for the juice and broken glass.

"No problem." She bent over Matthew and murmured to him. Incredibly he quieted. Carrie stroked his head and his eyes drooped.

Harrison wanted to ask how she did that, but was afraid any noise would set Matthew off again.

Instead he watched Carrie, with her fluorescent halo

and her blue-tipped fingers soothing his restless baby nephew.

No, she wasn't the typical White Oak Bayou resident, but she was warm and caring and on Thursday night, Harrison vowed to do his best to convince the other board members to see her as he did.

The unfortunate teenager selected to clean up the juice and broken glass arrived. Together, Harrison and Carrie walked down aisle ten, then back to the other end of aisle nine where Harrison put two cases of formula into his cart.

"You need anything else?" Carrie asked.

"Not that I know of." He couldn't help looking at the contents of her cart. Lettuce, yogurt, tofu—naturally—and low-fat single-serving frozen dinners. Except for the yogurt and tofu, it was a lot like his cart would normally look.

"Do you always shop in the middle of the night?"

"Mostly. It's when I get off work."

That made sense. "Do you have everything on your list?"

Carrie wrinkled her nose. "I don't have a list. I know I should, but I keep forgetting to make one." She laughed. "I'd probably lose it, anyway."

It occurred to Harrison that he was currently shopping without a list, as well. Mentally he ran through his day. "You know, on second thought, I could use a box of cereal. Nathan likes it a lot."

"Yeah, I know. Go ahead and get in the checkout line. I'll pick up a box for you."

Within five seconds of her departure, Matthew was whimpering again.

There was one checkout line and two people ahead of him. How could there be a line in the middle of the night? The woman in front of him had an entire grocery cart full of food. She glanced at Harrison, his crying nephew and two cases of formula, but didn't offer to let him go ahead of her.

Carrie joined him moments later and frowned at Matthew. "You can hear him all over the store."

She unstrapped Matthew from his carrier and lifted him, holding him close. Still frowning, she pressed her lips to his forehead. "He's awfully warm."

"Is he? He was okay earlier."

Carrie handed Harrison the baby. He *did* feel warm, but Harrison didn't know if it was too warm. How warm was too warm? When did warm become hot?

"What do you think?" he asked Carrie.

"I don't know." She touched Nathan, who had finished his juice and was dozing in the cart, then Matthew again. "He's a lot warmer than Nathan."

"Do you think he has a fever?" Harrison asked her, hoping she'd say no, but knowing she wouldn't.

Carrie nodded and bit her lip.

Harrison didn't know what to do with a feverish child. "He can't have a fever." But even in the greenish light, Matthew looked flushed. "He's not allowed to get sick. Not while I'm in charge."

"Oh, forever more. You young people today don't have the sense of a turnip," said a voice behind Harrison. "They make you get a license for everything but parenthood. I think it's high time they started licensing that, too."

It was the woman who had scolded him for bringing the boys out at night. She held out her arms. "Let me see that baby."

Responding to the voice of authority, Harrison handed Matthew to her.

She murmured soothingly as Carrie and Harrison looked at each other.

"He's teething," Harrison said because he felt compelled to demonstrate some shred of competence.

"That's it, then," said the woman with the loaded cart in front of them. She unsnapped a rubber band from a wad of coupons. "Mine always ran a fever when they were teething."

"A fever during teething is not normal," declared the cashier, and she and the other woman began arguing.

The grocery sacker, a grizzled man wearing a baseball cap, chuckled. "Give him a little whiskey in his milk, and he'll sleep right as rain."

"Whiskey's the best idea I've heard yet," Harrison said.

"You will *not* put whiskey in Matthew's bottle!" Carrie looked horrified.

"The whiskey is for me."

"He's only kidding," Carrie told the woman holding the baby.

Harrison said nothing as suggestions and comments about Matthew's fever, or lack of one, swirled around him. He was out of his element. Out of his area of expertise. Floundering.

He had a headache and had no trouble figuring out why. Ever since Nathan and Matthew had come to stay, Harrison's life had been broken into disorganized pieces. He hadn't been able to relax and enjoy a meal or sleep undisturbed. He felt horrible.

Maybe *he* was running a fever. Other people succumbed to viruses; he succumbed to disorganization.

Matthew was back in Carrie's arms. She and the woman were talking rashes while the woman unsnapped Matthew's pajamas and looked at his stomach.

"Yeah, chicken pox is going around," offered the cashier. The other woman was wheeling her groceries out.

"Chicken pox?" That was it. Harrison didn't care if he had to charter a helicopter to fly Stephanie back. Chicken pox would be beyond Jon's ability to cope.

"No rash," pronounced the woman. "He's probably just coming down with a cold."

Or pneumonia. Or some other dread disease. Harrison strapped Matthew back into his infant carrier and paid for the cereal, the formula, the cup and two empty bottles of juice. Was it his imagination, or had the baby grown warmer? And...weren't Nathan's cheeks looking flushed, too?

"Harrison?" Carrie pulled on his sleeve.

"What?"

"You've got that I'm-going-straight-to-the-emergency-room look on your face."

"With good reason," he admitted.

She half smiled and patted his shoulder. "Take the boys home. I'm right behind you."

Harrison wanted to tell her he could handle everything by himself, but not as much as he wanted her there with him. "Don't you have to write your reviews?" He was giving her an out, but he hoped she wouldn't take it.

"I'll write them later. Go on. You look beat."

And beat was exactly the way he felt after the nerve-racking drive home and wrestling the formula and the boys upstairs.

He was talking to Jon when Carrie knocked on the door. When she saw he was on the telephone, she quietly walked into the back and peeked in on Nathan before picking up Matthew and pacing with him.

Carrie's presence eased Harrison's mind more than talking with Jon did. He actually felt tension seep out of his shoulders and neck.

"Harrison?"

"Hmm?"

"Is someone there with you?" Jon asked.

"Uh, yeah. I ran into Carrie at the grocery store and she's here with Matthew now."

"*Is* she?"

"She baby-sat a few hours yesterday."

"*Did* she?"

"The kids like her."

"*Do* they?"

"Jon? I'm going to call the pediatrician now."

His brother laughed. "We'll talk later, won't we, Harrison?"

Harrison remembered his conversation with Felicia. Jon was in for more talking than he thought. "Absolutely."

After hanging up with Jon, Harrison called the answering service for the children's pediatrician, hating to wake him.

Then he and Carrie took turns pacing with Matthew while they waited for the doctor to call.

"Does he seem any worse?" Harrison asked.

"He's definitely got a fever." Carrie sat on the sofa and watched Harrison pace. "I hate that he can't tell us what's wrong."

"I hate being ineffective." Harrison stared down at his inconsolable baby nephew.

Carrie didn't say anything and when he looked at her, she had a softly tender expression on her face—

or as tender as a woman wearing black lipstick could look. "You're a good guy, Harry. You'll make a great dad."

And you'll make a great mother.

He didn't dare say the words even though he instinctively knew they were true. A man didn't say those words to a woman unless he was thinking of making her a mother. Carrie—a mother. His mind started darting into areas it should stay out of. "Parenthood is a huge responsibility," he murmured, going clammy at the thought.

"No kidding."

"You're great with the boys." He could say that, couldn't he?

"Thanks. I've never been around babies much before." She stared down at her hands. "I like it. They aren't concerned about your future, or your job, or whether you're living at a *proper* address."

Harrison stopped pacing and stared at her bent head. Now was not the time to mention the residents' board meeting agenda.

She was still speaking. "They don't care if you've had sixteen jobs since you left college, or that you changed majors four times and never graduated."

"Carrie?"

"Sorry," she mumbled. "I don't know where that came from."

"If I had to guess, I'd say you've been talking to your parents."

She made a face and nodded. "There was a message on my answering machine. They don't like me working nights."

"Do *you* like working nights?"

"I like this job," she answered slowly, as though

she had to give it some thought. "I've had it longer than most. The night part comes with it. Thank goodness this is a relatively safe area. If I didn't live here, I don't know. I'd probably have to find another job." She looked up at him with a small smile. "And it's not like I haven't done *that* before."

Before Harrison could think of a response, the telephone rang. It was the doctor.

"What did the he say?" Carrie asked, when Harrison hung up the phone.

"I'm supposed to bring Matthew in tomorrow morning. In the meantime, I should have taken his temperature, but I don't have a thermometer and I need some children's acetaminophen." He looked at her. "Would you—?"

"Go ahead." She stood. "I'll stay here."

Harrison shoved his wallet into his back pocket, and picked up his car keys. "The doctor suggested a cool bath, as well."

"Thanks, but I prefer warm ones."

He turned, his hand on the doorknob. "It's for Matthew."

Carrie gave him a look. "I know," she said gently. "It was a joke."

Grimacing, he pulled open the door. "I'm too tired for jokes."

Harrison returned to find Carrie putting Matthew in a fresh diaper.

"He really went for the cold bath. Not." She had little wet Matthew prints all over her T-shirt, which clung in interesting places. She'd either wiped off, or chewed off most of the dark lipstick, and she looked appealingly flustered. Very appealing.

Harrison frowned at the dark mark on Matthew's forehead. "Bruise?"

"Oh." Carrie wiped at it with the towel. "I kissed him."

"Lucky Matthew," he murmured.

Startled, Carrie looked up, bringing her now pink lips well within range of his. He leaned toward her.

"Harrison..."

"I know," he whispered. "But for right now, I want to pretend that I don't."

He kissed her gently, trying to acknowledge the shared emotions of the night and express his gratitude for her being there with him.

And, he just wanted an excuse to kiss her again.

The passion was still between them, but banked now. Even so, its warmth soothed his fraying nerves. "Thank you," he murmured when he broke the kiss.

Carrie nodded wordlessly, her cheeks as flushed as Matthew's.

Together, they followed the doctor's instructions and eventually, Matthew fell into a fitful sleep.

"Now it's your turn," Carrie said.

"I can't sleep. I've got to watch him. What if the medicine doesn't work?"

"You need the sleep and I'm used to staying up now anyway. I've still got to write my reviews. Why don't I go get my laptop and work right here?"

Harrison wanted to argue with her, but if he had to care for both boys all day tomorrow, then he needed sleep now. "Okay."

As he lay in his bed, he was conscious of Carrie in the next room. How did he feel about her? Was there anything behind the sizzle of a couple of kisses and gratitude for helping him out of a tight spot?

Did he want there to be?

Harrison honestly didn't know. He'd never had a relationship like this one, not that he was calling this a relationship. But he couldn't picture any of the women he'd dated babysitting and realized he hadn't known them all that well.

He'd never been as...domestically intimate with a woman as he'd been with Carrie. Laundry, grocery shopping, sick babies—and he still wanted to kiss her.

Go figure.

He fell asleep to the muted click of Carrie's computer keys as she tapped out her reviews.

Carrie stared at her computer screen where she'd typed "I will not fall in love with Harrison Rothwell" over and over. As appealingly human as he'd been the past several days, when he wasn't around children, he was as perfectly organized and as achievement-driven as her family. She'd never seen cabinets and drawers as organized as his were.

She'd been looking for rubber bands and had sought a kitchen junk drawer. Harrison didn't have a junk drawer. In contrast, all Carrie's drawers were junk drawers and that pretty much summed up the differences between them. They'd drive each other crazy.

She thought of the sweetly tender kiss he'd given her earlier. It was the sort of kiss that snuck past a woman's defenses, reached for her heartstrings and gave them a good yank.

Carrie drew a deep breath and resumed typing, but changed the "I will not fall in love with Harrison Rothwell" to "I will not become involved with Harrison Rothwell."

She was afraid it was too late for the other one.

CHAPTER SEVEN

A KNOCK on the bedroom door woke him up. "Harrison? It's eight-thirty."

Eight-thirty? He sat up and rubbed his eyes. "How's Matthew?"

"Cooler. I've made coffee for you. I'll bring it in, if you're decent," Carrie called from outside his door.

"Okay." He looked down at himself, hesitated, then said, "Let me put on a shirt."

"I've seen you without your shirt before." She stuck her head in, then walked into the room the rest of the way, carrying a cup. "I hope you like your coffee black."

"Black is fine." He could get used to being waited on like this.

"I called the pediatrician's office and they can see Matthew at nine-thirty."

"Great. You're fabulous."

"And don't you forget it." Carrie got as far as the trunk at the foot of the bed, looked at him and stopped.

He reached for the cup.

She did not hand it to him.

After a moment, Harrison dropped his arm and regarded her with raised eyebrows.

Carrie's eyes glazed. Her lips parted.

"Carrie?"

She blinked, then stared at the cup she held as if seeing it for the first time. "I—I'll just set it here and—and you can, uh..." She gestured with her hand as she backed away. "Whenever you're ready." Turning quickly, she fled the room.

Feeling a tweak of the old masculine pride, Harrison reached for his coffee. The sight of him without his shirt had flustered her. He smiled, then burned his tongue on the coffee.

She avoided his eyes when he came into the living room after showering. "I got Matthew all ready and packed the diaper bag for you. And I've kept a time log here, so you'll know how long it took me. I finished my reviews and thought that I'd run a load of laundry for the kids after Nathan wakes up—I'm babbling."

"I know." He couldn't prevent the smile from stealing across his face.

She drew a deep breath and finally met his eyes. "It's—probably the coffee. I made it stronger than I usually drink it."

She was embarrassed. Harrison didn't want her embarrassed, but how could he not be flattered? "The coffee was great. And I appreciate you bringing it to me." He felt guilty for adding the last, especially when color flooded her cheeks.

"There's more in the kitchen," she said, an artificially cheery note in her voice.

"Thanks. I'll pour myself another cup." Harrison was feeling unexpectedly cheery, himself. Carrie was obviously attracted to him. Since he was attracted to her as well, he was glad to know that it wasn't all one-sided. She was proving to be an unexpectedly interesting woman.

Normally Harrison was attracted to a woman who owned a Filofax and knew how to use it. And, yes, the women he dated were usually busy women with definite direction in their lives. The only difference among them had been the length of time they'd gone in his direction until the relationship reached a crossroads and they'd turned down a different path.

There'd never been any question of making permanent travel plans together.

Carrie's problem was that she couldn't decide the direction she wanted to travel and kept going down dead ends. He'd misjudged her, thinking she was one of those people who drifted through life without a plan. Harrison liked plans and goals, and couldn't tolerate drifters who fed off society without contributing anything to it. Yet, when he'd demonstrated the necessity for schedules and organization, she'd come through for him. Maybe all she'd needed was someone to show her the way.

Harrison had shown many people the way. That was his contribution to society.

He poured his coffee and watched her straighten the living room. Yes, when the boys were back with Jon and Stephanie, Harrison intended to explore his feelings for Carrie in greater depth.

"I'd better get Nathan ready," he said. "Thanks for all you've done, Carrie. I would have had a bad time if you hadn't helped me out."

She wrinkled her forehead. "Don't wake up Nathan. I can stay here and it'll be easier if you don't have to take him with you."

"I feel as though I've relied on you too much already."

"I don't mind."

"When will you sleep?"

"After you get back. A doctor's visit shouldn't take all day."

The thought of not having to wrestle with both boys proved to be an irresistible temptation.

Almost like Carrie, herself.

Harrison waited two hours before actually seeing the doctor. By the time he'd counted all the ducks cavorting around the walls of the examining room, fed Matthew the only bottle Carrie had packed and changed his diaper, Harrison was ready to hunt the man down and force him to see Matthew.

This was no way to run a business. They had an appointment for nine-thirty and the doctor wasn't even close. Was this how he kept his patients—forcing them to linger in a waiting room full of sick children spreading diseases to each other?

He was insulted. His time was as valuable as the doctor's. If ever a profession needed Harrison's time-management services, it was this one. But, when he complained to the receptionist, he was told that, like Matthew, other children had to be worked into the schedule.

"What schedule?" he snapped. "I see no evidence of a schedule!"

In response, she'd closed the frosted glass window between them.

It was past noon when he and Matthew finally made it back home. Poor Carrie. She must be exhausted.

He heard the now familiar "Sesame Street" music from outside the door. When he walked in, he saw Nathan sitting on the floor, plastic toys spread all around him.

The little boy saw Harrison and pointed to the television. "Big Bud."

"Yeah, Big Bird." Harrison failed to see the appeal of a giant yellow ostrich, but he wasn't going to argue.

He slung the diaper bag onto the floor and scanned the room. There was no sign of Carrie. Harrison's breathing quickened in alarm.

"Nathan, where's Carrie?"

The little boy pointed toward the sofa. "Carrie go night-night."

Walking with Matthew into the living room, Harrison peered over the back of the sofa to find Carrie asleep on the floor, a tower of sponge blocks by her head.

He stared down at her, unfamiliar feelings bombarding him. Guilt was a primary one. She'd given up a chunk of her time to help him and no one was more conscious of time than Harrison.

"Big Bud go bye-bye." Nathan hoisted himself to his feet and ran over to Carrie, squatted down and patted her head. "Cawee. Big Bud go bye-bye."

She roused immediately. "'Sesame Street's over already? Okay, lunchtime." She sat up, gasping when she saw Harrison. "How long have you been standing there?"

"A few minutes." He put the sleeping Matthew in his playpen.

"You should have said something. How's Matthew?"

"He's got a rip-roaring cold. I have instructions." Instructions involving medicine, a blue bulb he wasn't looking forward to using and the humidifier. "If he's not better in a few days, I get to take him back, or with any luck, his parents will.'' He followed Carrie and Nathan into the kitchen. ''I had to wait two hours. *Two hours.* And I wasn't the only one.''

As he told her about the doctor's visit, Carrie put on Nathan's bib and opened a can of ravioli, Nathan's current favorite food, to heat in the microwave. Harrison was standing in the doorway. With a start, he realized he should be getting Nathan ready for lunch instead of watching her do it. It was just that she seemed so competent and at ease.

''Hawee!''

He looked at his nephew. Nathan was bouncing his shoes on the high chair's footrest, a huge smile on his face.

''Hi.'' Harrison grinned back. He couldn't help it. One of those smiles from Nathan and the miserable morning at the pediatrician's wasn't quite as miserable.

He fell silent, wondering why a little boy's smile would affect him so.

Carrie brought Nathan a bowl of ravioli and he quivered in delight. She wrapped his fingers around a curved plastic spoon, while Nathan used his other hand to pick up ravioli and stuff it into his mouth.

''Nathan,'' she scolded without heat. ''Use your spoon.''

''Poon,'' Nathan dutifully repeated, and used it to stab ravioli, which he then picked up with his fingers.

Both Carrie and Harrison laughed.

''I'll fix him,'' Carrie said, and opened a jar of applesauce, which she poured into another bowl.

Nathan dropped his spoon, picked up the bowl and drank from it.

"Nathan, you'll never get ahead in business with those table manners," Harrison said.

"You won't get many dates, either." Carrie was writing on her schedule.

The schedule. Guilt washed over him. The boys were his responsibility, not hers. "Listen, Carrie. I know you're exhausted and I've been standing here letting you do all the work."

"I don't mind. Nathan and I had a good time this morning, didn't we, Nathan?"

At the sound of his name, Nathan looked up. He was wearing an applesauce beard. Harrison moistened a paper towel and wiped him off.

"This has been our day so far." Carrie handed Harrison the schedule, and walked around him to the far side of the bar. "Since I finished my reviews, I made up several scenarios for you, varying the number of children, their ages and whether a parent could be at home, or if both had outside jobs." She handed him a wad of papers. "I used your printer. I hope you don't mind."

"That's fine." Harrison was still scanning her morning activities. "You had time to do all this and the boys' laundry as well?"

Carrie nodded. "Nathan helped."

Nathan was mixing applesauce into his ravioli. "Nathan big boy," he said.

Smile or no, Harrison felt irritated. "I guess you're finished," he said and took the bowls away.

Nathan wailed, arms outstretched.

The pitch of Nathan's cries stabbed Harrison straight through to a place in his psyche that shrieked for him to stop the noise at any cost.

He gave him the bowls back. Nathan promptly

stuffed a handful of applesauce-covered ravioli into his mouth.

"I always thought canned ravioli could use a little punching up, myself." Carrie grinned, and stuck her hands into the back pockets of her jeans. "So what do you think of the schedules?"

Happy to avoid watching Nathan eat, Harrison glanced down at them. Though they incorporated no known Rothwell rules, there were bits and pieces that he might find useful. "You've put in a lot of work," he said. More work than he felt comfortable with her doing. They had no agreement, formal or otherwise.

"Well, I just had all these ideas and they sort of bubbled out." She peeled back three pages and pointed. "Felicia particularly liked this one."

Something about the way she spoke told him she wasn't referring to Monday night. "When did you talk with Felicia?"

"Oh, she called a couple of hours ago. I meant to tell you."

"Here? She called me here?"

"She called your office first, she said. Anyway, we talked, and she said you don't have to call her back."

Harrison tamped down his temper. "What did you talk about?"

"The *schedules*."

Carefully he set the papers on the kitchen bar. "And you didn't feel you should discuss them with me first?"

"You weren't here."

Harrison caught himself just as he was about to deliver a lecture like the one he'd give an employee who'd ignored protocol. Carrie wasn't an employee, and the sooner both she and Felicia realized it, the better.

He could make his point now, one that would surely leave her angry and hurt, or ignore it because Stephanie would be back to pick up the boys on Friday. After that, he and Carrie wouldn't be working together. In fact, he shouldn't have a reason to call her again.

All this raced through his mind while Carrie looked at him, obviously hoping for his approval. He couldn't disappoint her, not after all she'd done. "Just on first reading, the schedules look impressive. I'll study them when Nathan takes his nap. Thanks."

When she smiled, he knew he'd said the right thing.

"Let me know if you need any more help," she said, still smiling as she picked up her laptop.

Harrison walked her to the door. "I'm not going to be able to pay you back now as it is."

She turned. "I enjoyed being with the boys."

At that moment, Nathan threw one of his bowls on the floor. Harrison groaned. "I hope that was empty."

Laughing, Carrie opened the door. "And I will enjoy leaving you to clean up the mess."

After she left, Harrison realized he hadn't told her about the vote on her eviction. Never mind. If all went as he intended, she need never know about it.

After cleaning the kitchen, Harrison spent the rest of Nathan's nap time redoing all Carrie's schedules. Not that he doubted they'd work, but he wanted more than working, he wanted efficiency. He wanted a household than ran so well, it could absorb crises such as an unexpected illness, or sitter problems, without everything falling into chaos.

He also wanted his schedules based on *Rothwell's Rules*. That was the whole point, wasn't it?

He still smarted over Felicia's "more idealistic than practical" crack. He resented her speaking to Carrie without speaking to him.

And he resented Carrie being able to whip out work that would take him days to generate.

He wasn't proud of his feelings, but there they were. He wasn't thrilled knowing that he'd needed help this week, either. How on earth did single parents cope?

A sleepy Nathan walked into the room. "Cawee?"

"She's home asleep." Harrison thought a moment. "Carrie went night-night."

Nathan walked around the room anyway. Harrison scrambled to put up his papers. Normally he'd file them, but he'd have to get to that later. Right now, it was obvious that Nathan was not at all happy about Carrie's absence. Hoping to avoid an outbreak of tears, Harrison headed for the kitchen. "Want some juice?"

Nathan followed him and Matthew stirred. Good. Time for Harrison to put his own plan into effect.

His own plan didn't work. For one thing, Nathan wasn't interested in staying inside the living room. Harrison could hardly blame him. He was getting a case of cabin fever, himself.

Therefore, instead of sorting his mail, or filing, he took the boys outside. Across the parking lot, there was a jogging trail that followed the banks of the bayou. Nathan didn't want to follow the jogging trail. He wanted to run too close to the bayou and give his uncle Harrison heart failure. He also wanted to pick up rocks, grass, twigs, weeds and trash and put them into his mouth.

Harrison tried to put him into the stroller with Matthew, but Nathan screamed, "No!" and ran away. Harrison followed, pushing the stroller.

Matthew didn't appreciate the bouncy ride and began to cry.

Harrison caught Nathan around the waist and sat him in the stroller—or he tried to. Nathan stiffened his legs, all the while screaming, "No!" Eventually Harrison got him in, but his kicking hurt Matthew, who was seated in front of him.

Harrison was forced to pick up Nathan, who continued to struggle, and wheel Matthew back through the parking lot as fast as he could.

The concrete and steel around the outside elevator magnified the boys' cries.

Fortunately Carrie's tiny apartment was at the other end of the hall, not that she could possibly sleep through this.

"Mr. Rothwell?" An elderly woman stepped outside her door. "What is going on?"

"I'm baby-sitting my nephews." He concentrated on the elevator as if his will alone could part the doors.

"My Wednesday afternoon bridge group is here. We can't concentrate on our play."

"Sorry, Mrs. Garner," he muttered and hoisted Nathan into a better position.

She stared at him until the elevator came.

"Does she think I'm doing this on purpose?" he grumbled to himself.

Nathan's crying continued long after Harrison got them back inside.

Dinner was a disaster. Bath time was a calamity. Forget the bedtime story. Nathan threw the book at the playpen. If Matthew had been in it, he could have been hurt.

Harrison, to his shame, lost his temper and yelled. Nathan yelled louder.

And there was a knock at the door. Actually a pounding.

Carrie. It had to be. Harrison exhaled in relief. "I'm glad you're here—"

A disapproving Mrs. Garner stood at the door. "You have failed to quiet these children."

"I'm doing my best," Harrison protested.

"You must let them know who's in charge, Mr. Rothwell."

"Oh, I think they know exactly who's in charge," he said dryly.

In the silence after his remark, Nathan wandered into the foyer. The cloth feet of his pajamas slipped on the tile and he sat heavily, prompting a fresh set of sobs.

"I live in White Oak because I do not wish to be disturbed by crying children."

Harrison picked up Nathan. "I can appreciate that, but—"

"Therefore, I am lodging a complaint to the board."

Harrison stared at her. "I'm on the board."

"I am aware of that. I'm complaining to you."

Sarcasm overcame good sense. "And you want me to report myself?"

Mrs. Garner tightened her mouth. "I've already spoken to the others."

Great. They wouldn't be predisposed to grant fa-

vors tomorrow night. "Excuse me," Harrison said
tightly. "I need to see to the boys." And he shut the
door.

After only a few minutes of walking, Nathan quieted and stuck his thumb into his mouth. A few
minutes more and his eyes shut. Without changing the
cadence of his stride, Harrison walked into the back
bedroom and laid him on the bed. His chest was damp
where Nathan's head had been and moisture had
formed curls at the base of the toddler's head.
Harrison decided to cover him up later.

Once his brother fell asleep, Matthew did as well.

Harrison surveyed the ruins of his once-neat living
room and wondered how Carrie had managed everything.

And then he broke with his evening routine, turned
out the light and abandoned the mess.

CHAPTER EIGHT

CRYING woke him.

Harrison headed for the playpen in the living room
before realizing that it was Nathan who was crying.

Flipping on the light in the spare bedroom, Harrison
saw the toddler had the same blazing red cheeks
Matthew had had yesterday. "Aw, Nathan, not you,
too. No wonder you were so cranky." He reached for
him, and drew a sharp breath.

His little body felt like it was on fire. It must be
ten times hotter than Matthew's had been. Nathan was
so hot, it frightened Harrison. His hands went cold,
making Nathan's skin seem hotter by contrast.

He picked up Nathan and carried him to the phone.
Without thinking about it, he called the one person he
trusted—the one person he knew would help. The one
person awake at three-thirty in the morning.

Yes, he should be handling crises like this himself,
but Nathan was sick and all bets were off. This was
no time for pride or for proving a point.

Carrie answered on the second ring.

"Nathan's sick," Harrison said, without even saying hello.

"I'll be right up." She hung up the phone.

Harrison unlocked the front door, then stripped off
Nathan's pajamas.

Carrie was at his door in less than a minute. She
must have run all the way. Knocking once before

coming inside, she asked breathlessly, "Have you taken his temperature?"

"Not yet." This time, Harrison knew to do so before calling the doctor. "The thermometer is in the bathroom."

"I'll get it," she said, already running down the hall.

Harrison carried Nathan into his bedroom, Carrie right behind him.

"I'll take his temperature, then get him into a cool bath. You call the doctor," she said. Her voice was calm and soothing. She was organized and in control. They made a great team.

Harrison dressed while he went through the call-and-wait procedure with the doctor, already guessing what he'd say. Amazing. One sick child and already he knew the drill.

Carefully writing down the correct dose of acetaminophen for Nathan, Harrison listened to the doctor's instructions and discovered he'd anticipated correctly. He *was* getting the hang of this parenting stuff. He was also getting the hang of parenting worry.

Grabbing the medicine, he headed toward the bathroom where he could hear Nathan screaming, the sound amplified by the tile.

"I'm sorry, Nathan," Carrie was saying over and over. She held him in the cool water, scooping more over his shoulders, tears streaming down her face. "I *hate* this," she said when she saw Harrison.

"I do, too." He gripped her shoulder in sympathy. "I'm glad I'm not going through this alone."

She sniffed.

Heedless of the wet, Harrison sat on the edge of

the bathtub. "Do you think we can get medicine down him yet?"

"Not when he's this upset," she said. Wrapping Nathan in a towel, she took him out of the tub and cradled him to her. "I know I'm supposed to let him air dry, but I just can't." She bent her head and cuddled the crying toddler.

Harrison stared down at her, at her dark curls and tearstained cheeks, at the way she murmured to Nathan—at her bare feet. She hadn't even taken the time to put on shoes. She probably hadn't even locked her door.

Outwardly he didn't move, but inside, he was in turmoil as his emotions underwent a profound realignment.

In his mind's eye, he could see future scenes exactly like this one with Carrie holding and soothing another child. A child with dark curly hair and the Rothwell smile.

Their child.

Harrison had never considered children in such an immediate way before. He'd always assumed he would marry and have children someday, but the emphasis had been on *someday*. Maybe it was because he'd never met anyone he could imagine linking himself to for the rest of his life, let alone having children with. The women he dated didn't have time for children.

But Carrie was made to be a mother, not a dedicated career woman. He wondered if she realized it yet.

Harrison looked farther into the future, and saw Carrie driving a minivan full of kids, saw Carrie taking on the school board, saw Carrie *running* the school board. She'd be an activist mother, fiercely fighting to improve the world for her children—their children.

She'd have a Filofax, all right, because that would be the only way she'd keep track of all her activities and the kids' schedules. He could help her with that. He'd sensed that she lacked direction and now he knew that children would provide that direction. What she'd seen as a flaw—many different jobs and studies—would provide a rich background for raising children.

Scenes flashed through his mind like pages from a parenting manual: Carrie at the kitchen table helping their son with homework, Carrie braiding their daughter's hair, Carrie sewing Halloween costumes.

And where was Harrison in all this?

By necessity, he'd spend the majority of his day at work, and he vowed that he'd be successful enough at it so that his children would have a mother who was available to them. He'd supply the grounding and the support—the basics. Sweet, sensitive, unpredictable Carrie would bring the color into their lives.

For the first time, he completely understood why his sister-in-law stayed at home with Nathan and Matthew, and why Jon encouraged her.

Nathan had quieted. "I think you can try the medicine now," Carrie suggested.

Harrison measured pink liquid into the special spoon. His hand shook slightly. It wasn't surprising, considering he was in the throes of a personal epiphany.

Nathan let Harrison pour the spoon into his mouth, then pushed it away. "No!" Medicine dribbled down his chin.

"Swallow, Nathan." Harrison scooped it back up and tried again.

Carrie held Nathan's head still as he struggled with his legs and arms. "Maybe he has a sore throat."

"I hope not." Harrison eyed the pink stains on the towel. "Do you think we got enough down him?"

"I don't know. Any is bound to help. We don't want to overdose him."

Harrison stared at his nephew, feeling the same helplessness he'd felt when dealing with Matthew. "The doctor said if the fever isn't down within an hour we should call back."

"Poor baby. He's sick, he's in a strange place and his mommy and daddy aren't here." Carrie looked up at Harrison, fresh tears in her eyes.

At that moment, Harrison fell in love with her. Maybe he'd been falling for a while, but at this instant, he knew he'd landed. "He's in the next best place." His voice had a gruffness catching at it.

Fortunately Carrie didn't seem to notice.

Now wasn't the time to share his new knowledge and not only because they were busy dealing with Nathan.

This week had been out of the ordinary for both of them. Harrison's life had been completely disrupted by his nephews. He and Carrie needed "normal" time—time together without Matthew and Nathan. Time to explore their feelings for each other.

It was the only part of the future that he couldn't see clearly, and that was because he hadn't spent any time alone with her.

"You know what you need? A rocking chair," Carrie said, prompting a vision of her in a long, soft nightgown, rocking a baby.

He was becoming sickeningly sentimental. Next thing he knew, he'd be sprinkling rose petals on their marriage bed.

Marriage bed. Marriage. He mentally tested the word and found it didn't evoke the same dead-end feelings it used to.

No, marriage to Carrie would be a beginning.

They spent the next couple of hours taking turns sitting on Nathan's bed and rocking him. His temperature fell and he eventually went back to sleep.

In contrast, Harrison was wide-awake and reluctant for Carrie to leave, even though he knew she had to work.

They walked down the hall together while he thought of an excuse to keep her there. "How about some breakfast? I can scramble a mean egg."

"Eggs are bad for you."

"Eggs have gotten a bum rap."

They reached the living room and Carrie hesitated. "I have toast," Harrison offered. "Plenty of cereal…"

That prompted a laugh. "I can't eat Nathan's cereal. I'll go for the eggs. I haven't had any in ages."

They spoke in whispers to keep from waking Matthew, who had miraculously slept through Nathan's trauma, and it created the illusion of intimacy, which was fine with Harrison.

Withdrawing a carton of eggs, he prepared to create one of his two culinary masterpieces for Carrie, the other being French toast. But he didn't have the right bread for that.

Carrie sat on a bar stool and propped her chin on her hand.

With newly heightened awareness, Harrison knew

something was bothering her and he didn't think it was only Nathan. "Long night?" he asked.

"I've been out later on nights after the clubs close at two a.m. and the band decides to jam. That's when they play their new stuff and I can get an idea of where they're headed musically." She drew a deep breath and let it out in a slow sigh. "I probably should have stayed late this evening, but I didn't."

Harrison cracked eggs into a bowl, hoping Carrie was impressed that he was doing it with one hand. "Lucky for me."

"You would have been okay. You've already been through it all with Matthew. Speaking of which, I'll stay with him while you take Nathan to the doctor."

Harrison added a pinch of oregano to the eggs. "I might want to take Matthew with me. If I've got two crying kids, maybe the doctor will see us faster."

Carrie laughed, but it wasn't her normal, uninhibited Carrie laugh.

"I can't keep imposing and I know you need to write your reviews."

"Ugh." She covered her face with her hands. "*Please* let me stay with Matthew. I don't want to write anything."

Harrison beat the eggs. "Was the band that bad?"

"I honestly don't know whether they were or not," she said, dropping her hands. "I should hear them again, but I don't want to. The thing is, when I first started reviewing, I would have loved them and written a review full of adjectives and all that. But lately, I don't know." She was silent for a moment. "I don't seem to be as 'into' the club scene as I was and I shouldn't write a bad review just because I've lost my enthusiasm."

She didn't look like part of the club scene right now, with her bare feet, nondescript jeans, shirt and vest. And the traces of her lipstick indicated that she'd worn a normal red color.

Silently Harrison rejoiced. Carrie working nights wasn't conducive to a relationship.

She moaned, catching him by surprise. "It's starting again. I can feel it."

"What?" He got out a skillet and dropped a chunk of butter into it. It was a smaller chunk than he normally used, in deference to Carrie.

She didn't comment on the butter, but unhappiness drew her eyebrows together. "Every job I've ever had, I start out and think, 'This is it. This is the one. I've found my calling.' Everything goes along fine and then I get that niggling 'not right' feeling."

"What do you mean?"

"Oh…" She bunched her shoulders then dropped them. "Just a feeling that I should be doing something else. I guess you could say that I'm searching for a sense of destiny."

"I always knew what I wanted to be," he told her. "I had a knack for managing and organizing that other people didn't." Harrison had taken a psychology course or two himself and was deliberately sharing his feelings with her. It was an important step in building a relationship. They'd taken some of the steps out of order, but that didn't mean they couldn't go back and fill in.

"You're lucky." She shook her head. "I really thought this job was what I was meant to do. I've worked at it longer than I've ever worked at a job. I tell myself that all jobs have their good times and their not-so-good times, but eventually, I realize the job is wrong for me.''

"There are people who make a career out of working as temps. Their adaptability is an asset.''

"Been there, done that.''

Harrison smiled. "Then maybe you're ready for a break.'' Say a break long enough to raise a few children?

"I've tried that before, when I can afford to. I've also forced myself to keep working past the time I want to quit a job. I end up quitting anyway. What's wrong with me?'' There was a pleading look in her eyes.

Harrison got out a Parmesan cheese grater. "Nothing is wrong with you. When you find what you want to do with your life, you'll know it.''

"I'm twenty-seven years old. Isn't it time I figured out what I want to be when I grow up?''

Harrison could suggest aptitude tests and career counseling, but something told him that wasn't what she wanted to hear. Besides, he had his own ideas on what she could do with her life, though it wasn't the right time to mention them. He fell back on platitudes. "Everyone is different, Carrie.''

He could tell she was mildly disappointed that he hadn't gifted her with any words of wisdom.

"Yeah. Whatever. I'll bet you're sorry you asked me for breakfast, right?''

He turned the wheel on the grater. "I'm flattered that you felt comfortable enough to share your feelings with me.'' And he was, but "share'' and "feelings'' were words women liked to hear, and Harrison was not above using them on Carrie.

She watched him. "What are you doing?''

"Freshly grating Parmesan for my special Eggs Italiano. Prepare to be amazed."

He didn't know if she was amazed or not, but Carrie ate the eggs, and she did stay with Matthew while Harrison took Nathan to the pediatrician.

Once again, he shot the better part of a day in the doctor's waiting room.

Since today he'd planned to take the boys to their nursery school and stop by his office, he had to call Sharon and tell her he was staying at home with a sick child.

"You have a pile of messages three feet high," she informed him.

"Sorry. Can't do anything about it. Delegate what you can and prioritize the rest for me. I'll call you back this afternoon."

"Ooh, delegation. That's an executive responsibility, isn't it?"

"That's why you're an executive secretary."

"So I am."

She was angling for executive assistant and they both knew it. Harrison had not seriously considered promoting Sharon because it seemed as if a week didn't go by without her being late, or leaving early or being on the phone dealing with some incident involving her children.

Harrison truly sympathized with her, now more than ever, but he needed someone who was going to be there for him one-hundred percent.

When he published the *Domestic Primer*, he was going to give her the first copy.

It was a matter of organization, he knew it with every fiber of his being. Even with both Matthew and Nathan catching colds this week, Harrison knew if he'd had a chance to prepare for the eventuality, he wouldn't be taking the day off.

After he got back home and Carrie had left, he worked at incorporating her schedules with his—a blending of the best of Carrie's innovations and *Rothwell's Rules of Time Management.*

Next, he returned phone calls while the boys napped. They took longer naps than usual, probably because of the disruption to their sleep schedule.

About three o'clock, Harrison felt completely drained. Stretching out on the sofa, he prepared to take a short nap, himself—short, because he expected either Matthew or Nathan to wake up momentarily.

Harrison slept until a plaintive, "Hawee joose?" woke him up.

"Sure, Nathan." He sat up, feeling as though he'd gone through a harder than normal workout. Glancing at the playpen, he saw that Matthew was awake as well, but was quietly playing with the soft toys around him.

Harrison focused on his watch. "Six o'clock! Guys, you must be hungry." And wide-awake, he thought. No eight-thirty bedtime tonight.

Harrison gave his nephews their medicine, fixed dinner and launched into an evening routine of sorts. He and Nathan were making a game of picking up the living room—one of Carrie's suggestions—when Harrison saw the pile of mail and papers. He hadn't even gone to his mailbox for today's mail yet.

Picking up Matthew and a couple of his favorite toys, Harrison started down the hall. "Come on, Nathan. Want to go play file in Uncle Harrison's room?"

Nathan, finger in his mouth, followed him. He was

subdued, but Harrison was relieved to see him feeling better.

"Okay, buddy, you're going be filing in the old circular file, there." Harrison pointed to a wastepaper basket and gave Nathan an empty envelope. He set Matthew on the carpet with a stuffed elephant nearby, which he promptly put into his mouth.

Harrison's work papers were mixed with the household papers. Another Rothwell rule broken. He separated the stack and there, on top of the household mail, was the Residents' Board Meeting agenda.

He sucked the breath between his teeth to keep from saying the first word that popped into his mind, and which Nathan would probably repeat.

Today was Thursday. The board meeting was tonight. How could he have forgotten? What time was it? His bedside clock read 7:42.

Harrison stared. The meeting had begun at seven.

He'd never forgotten a meeting in his life.

Nathan pulled at the electric bill and dropped it into the trash. "Der."

Nathan. Matthew. Harrison racked his fingers through his hair. Even if he'd remembered the meeting, he'd made no plans for anyone to watch the boys. It had never occurred to him. That he could make such an oversight was beyond comprehension.

Nathan picked up an advertisement from a brokerage firm and threw it at the wastebasket. "Na-tun big boy."

"And Uncle Harrison is an idiot."

"Hawee ut," Nathan repeated solemnly.

"You betcha." No, he hadn't called a baby-sitter since that first day because he'd had Carrie, who was gone by now. He relied on her far too much, even allowing for the fact that he was brand-new to parenting. And all she'd asked in return was—

Carrie's eviction. The board was voting on Carrie's eviction. Harrison brought a hand to his forehead as he tried to gather his thoughts. "Nathan, we've got to go bye-bye." He scooped Matthew up and hurried to the living room.

"Bye-bye?" Nathan ran after him as fast as he could.

"Yes, bye-bye." Harrison quickly unfolded the stroller and set Matthew in, then Nathan in the seat behind. "I'm sorry, Nathan," he apologized, feeling like scum. "I know you don't feel well, and I wouldn't do this if it weren't an emergency."

Without so much as a glance at his reflection, Harrison quickly pushed the boys out the door and to the elevator.

Maybe the board hadn't voted on Carrie, yet. Meetings frequently lasted two or more hours. He jabbed the elevator button until the car arrived.

Racing out of the elevator, he jogged down the sidewalk to the community building and burst in. Wheeling the stroller down the aisle of metal folding chairs to the front table, he ignored the openmouthed expressions on the faces of the other board members and parked the stroller behind his chair.

"Sorry, I'm late. I was unavoidably detained."

"Hawee ut," Nathan said into the silence that followed Harrison's arrival.

Harrison blinked, smiled and declined to translate.

"Mr. Rothwell, we'd given up on you." Mrs. Greenborough was board president.

"I'm here now, Mrs. Greenborough." He smiled

at the matron in the knit suit and diamond-encrusted knuckles.

"We knew you were here because your car was in the parking lot." The speaker was J.G. Ottwell, perennially dressed in white shoes, slacks and knit shirt so he could play eighteen holes of golf at a moment's notice. "But you were not present at this meeting."

J.G. frequently got on his nerves. Tonight wasn't any different. "As I said, I was detained." Harrison dropped the "unavoidably" since he didn't believe himself capable of lying twice.

The two other members of the board just looked at him as though an alien had landed in their midst.

Under the guise of shuffling through the papers at his place, Harrison's gaze swept the room. The meeting was lightly attended, for which he was grateful, but even a swift glance was enough to tell him that every eye in the place was staring right at him.

What was the matter with everybody? So he was late. Very late. So he wasn't dressed in a suit. Big deal. Why didn't they fill him in on what they were discussing and just get on with the meeting?

And he didn't like the way they were ignoring the boys. He gestured to them. "These are my nephews. They're visiting me for the week."

"We know." Mrs. Greenborough very deliberately spread three sheets of paper in front of her. "The board has received complaints about disturbing noises."

Mrs. Garner glared at him from the second row. She'd been busy.

"As you can appreciate, that places us in an extremely awkward position. We'd been discussing that very thing prior to your arrival."

For more than forty-five minutes? Harrison glanced at the copies of the complaint letters and was mildly surprised to see that they had come from different people. Other than Mrs. Garner, no one had bothered to contact him, not that he could have done much.

Out of the corner of his eyes, he saw Nathan fidget. "I apologize for any awkwardness. My sister-in-law is returning tomorrow and will be picking up the boys then and that should resolve the matter."

"Mr. Rothwell." Mrs. Greenborough laced her fingers together on the table in front of her. "The White Oak Bayou Condominiums is a haven of solitude in the shadow of downtown Houston. What we have is precious and must be preserved at all costs. Children are not allowed to live here."

"Hawee...out."

With difficulty, Harrison maintained his composure. "Matthew and Nathan are only visiting me. For one week. They aren't living here. I've noticed other children visiting."

Mrs. Greenborough picked up one of the complaint letters. "Crying and screaming for hours during the night," she read. She looked over her glasses at him. "I suggest to you that your nephews did not wish to visit."

"Unfortunately the boys both came down with fevers and were a little cranky."

"You mean you brought sick children here to expose all of us?"

People recoiled as though Harrison were spreading bubonic plague. "Not on purpose," he snapped. "But there was no one else to watch them."

He had to get out of his chair and intercept Nathan,

who was about to climb out of the stroller. "Stay in the stroller, Nathan."

"No!"

Harrison wasn't going to get into an unwinnable argument and noisy struggle in front of everyone. Instead he sat down with Nathan on his lap. "I've apologized for any disturbances and I've told you that the boys will be leaving tomorrow. Can we please get on with the meeting so I can put the boys to bed?"

"Very well." Mrs. Greenborough cleared her throat and managed to convey extreme disapproval. "There is a motion on the floor to censure Harrison Rothwell for violating standing rule four, subsection b of the White Oak Bayou Residents' Agreement. Is there further discussion?"

"Wait a minute," Harrison protested. "Isn't censuring extreme?"

"You violated the rules, Mr. Rothwell." Mrs. Greenborough pointed to Nathan with her pen. "There's the proof."

"So you are saying that children cannot visit residents here?"

"We have been discussing establishing a visitation rule." She made it sound like prison. "As our policy now stands, quiet children may visit. Children who scream in the middle of the night violate the disturbance rule."

"I call for the question," said J.G.

He was really getting on Harrison's nerves now. Why didn't anybody cite him for driving his golf cart all over the complex?

"All those in favor of citing Harrison Rothwell say 'aye.'"

Four voices answered "aye."

"Opposed?" asked Mrs. Greenborough.

"Nay," Harrison said, thinking dark thoughts.

"The 'ayes' have it and Mr. Rothwell will be mailed the citation."

"Just hand the damn thing to me!"

"Dam," Nathan said clearly.

Mrs. Greenborough's eyebrows lifted. "There are procedures that must be followed."

Right now, Harrison didn't want to follow any procedures. He wanted to take Nathan and Matthew home. Glancing behind him, he was grateful to see that Matthew was asleep.

Continuing the meeting, Mrs. Greenborough droned on. Harrison handed Nathan his expensive gold pen and let him scribble all over the complaint letters. The scratching sound was loud and annoyed Mrs. Greenborough.

Harrison smiled inwardly.

"The next item on the agenda is the eviction of Carrie Brent."

"Cawee!" Nathan smiled at Harrison.

"I move we strike the item from the agenda," Harrison said.

There was no second.

"Okay, then I move we rescind the citation for displaying nonstandard planters. She removed them when asked."

"Just because a violation is no longer being practiced does not mean it never occurred."

"In view of the fact that this citation makes her tenth, and thus prompts the eviction question, I believe citing her is extreme."

"On what grounds?"

Harrison was thankful that he'd prepared his arguments in advance. He only wished he'd remembered to bring his notes. "Nonstandard application of rules."

Mrs. Greenborough bristled. "To what are you referring?"

"In layman's terms, we're picking on her." He nodded to the man next to him. "J.G., here, drives his golf cart across the parking lot and parks it in a visitor's spot instead of leaving it in the area specifically set aside for golf carts, and we've never cited him."

"It's way on the other side of the complex!" J.G. protested.

"It's still a violation of the rules. And every morning, the poodle in 312 runs loose. The residents' agreement clearly states that pets must be kept on a leash. I've checked the files and we've issued no citation."

"We cannot act when we have not received complaints."

"Why not? The board has initiated complaints against Carrie before."

Harrison felt all eyes upon him. Gazes that had previously been annoyed turned malevolent.

Mrs. Greenborough spoke, "And do you wish to issue a complaint, Mr. Rothwell?" Ice formed around each precisely enunciated syllable.

"No, but I could, which is my point. If we applied our rules to ourselves as stringently as we apply them to Carrie, then it would be like living in a police state."

"Point of order," one of the other board members said. "We have a motion with no second."

"I'd like to continue the discussion," Harrison said. "Will someone please second my motion?"

"You are out of order, Mr. Rothwell." Mrs. Greenborough looked up and down the table.

No one spoke. The only sound was the scratching Nathan made as he scraped Harrison's pen across the tabletop. Harrison fully expected to be cited for destruction of board property.

"Motion dies for lack of a second," she said.

"Oh, come on!" Harrison bellowed.

"The next order of business is the matter of Carrie Brent's eviction."

"We're opening ourselves to a lawsuit." Harrison had hoped he wouldn't have to use this argument. "She'll cite discrimination."

"I've not called for discussion. Please follow procedure, Mr. Rothwell."

As Harrison's frustration grew, so did Nathan's fidgeting. He was now bored with destroying Harrison's pen and decorating the tabletop. Harrison withdrew the only other object he thought might interest Nathan: his keys.

"Is there any discussion?"

"Unless we apply our regulations uniformly, Carrie Brent will sue us for discrimination," Harrison repeated. He hoped they'd listen to him because he didn't know how much longer he could control Nathan.

The woman board member at the far end of the table gestured to Mrs. Greenborough. After a whispered consultation, Mrs. Greenborough turned to him. "I've been advised that Miss Brent has been observed entering and leaving your home at odd hours."

"So?"

After raising her eyebrows, Mrs. Greenborough flipped through the Residents' Policy and Procedure Manual. "We could evict her solely for violating section twenty-two."

"What?"

"Matters of moral turpitude."

As the full meaning of their implication sank in, Harrison felt himself losing the last hold he had on his temper. "She works nights. And instead of sending sanctimonious letters to the board when she heard the crying, she came upstairs to see if she could help." He'd already lost, he knew, but he was going to appeal to their consciences, in the event they had any left. "She was the only one to do so and I am thankful she did. Most of you have grown children. Has it been so long since they were babies that you can't remember what it was like the first time they got sick and you were scared and you didn't know what to do?"

He stood, holding up a fussy Nathan. "This little boy had a temperature of a hundred and three last night. He should be home in bed. So, go ahead and take your vote, Mrs. Greenborough."

"All in favor of evicting Carrie Brent due to ten violations of the Residents' Agreement signify by saying 'aye.'"

Harrison stared at the board members.

"Aye," they said.

"Eye," said Nathan and poked his eye.

Harrison pulled his hand down.

"All opposed?"

"Nay," Harrison said firmly, already putting Nathan back into the stroller.

"Nay," Nathan said.

"Motion carried, and papers to evict will be served."

Harrison flipped over an agenda and scribbled on it. His pen wouldn't work due to Nathan's scratching the tip on the table, so he grabbed J.G.'s out of his hand. "According to the policy you all love to cite, Carrie can file an appeal, which must be discussed at the next board meeting." He wheeled the stroller in front of the table and handed the scrawled note to Mrs. Greenborough. "Consider this her appeal."

CHAPTER NINE

CARRIE was going to be thrown out of her home and it was all his fault. Day after day, or rather night after night, she'd been there for him and the one thing she'd asked in return, he'd been unable to give her.

Harrison was thoroughly disgusted with himself. This whole week had been like riding a roller coaster in the dark—he knew the twists and turns were coming, but he couldn't see when to brace himself for them.

His normal routine had been shattered and the results were disastrous. His work week was a near total loss, even accounting for the notes on the domestic primer. Meetings had been postponed, phone calls never returned and Friday's staff meeting had been postponed until Monday. Never in the history of Rothwell Time Management Consultants, Inc., had Harrison not held a Friday staff meeting or delegated someone to hold it for him.

And as for this latest debacle... How could he have allowed himself to be underprepared for the board meeting, let alone have it slip his mind? Under normal circumstances, he would have dressed in a dark suit and arrived early to chitchat with the others. He would have created a brilliant argument to be delivered in an offhandedly casual way, as though he'd just thought of it. He would have wooed the board, rather than hit them over the head.

Instead he'd arrived late, wearing a shirt stained

with pink medicine and relied on rough notes from memory.

He'd alienated the board and all the members present. Yes, he'd filed an appeal, but it was just a formality. All he'd done was buy her an extra month before she was voted out for good.

After putting Matthew and Nathan to bed, Harrison tried to figure out how to break the news to Carrie.

She wouldn't be home for hours and he hoped he was asleep by then. Neither did he want to leave a message on her answering machine, but he wouldn't put it past one of the board members to do so.

Harrison decided to wait until tomorrow morning. By then, he would have had a chance to develop a plan to approach the board.

But the next morning, he didn't call her. She would just be going to bed. Why disturb her sleep? he rationalized to himself.

He and the boys spent a subdued morning where Harrison didn't accomplish much, but didn't lose any ground, either. Today was the day his cleaning lady came and Harrison was overjoyed at the thought of regaining his pristine home.

Stephanie arrived at two o'clock, smack in the middle of nap time. Just the sight of his sister-in-law made Harrison breathe easier. Now things would get back to normal.

"So how was being a parent for a week?" she asked, tiptoeing over to the playpen, a longing expression on her face as she saw the sleeping Matthew.

"Have you talked to Jon yet?" Harrison countered.

Stephanie quietly retreated from the playpen. "I

called, but he's in a seminar and I didn't want to disturb him.''

Great. He'd get to break bad news twice in one day. ''Well, it's like this.'' Harrison recapped the highlights—or the lowlights—of the week for his sister-in-law.

Her face crumpled. ''They were sick and I wasn't here?'' she wailed.

''Just colds and I took them to the doctor. They're much better now.''

Stephanie ran down the hallway to check on Nathan.

With an understanding borne of experience, Harrison patiently went to his pantry and began packing leftover food, bibs and baby dishes. When Stephanie returned he gestured for her to join him in the kitchen.

She was crying. ''I shouldn't have gone.''

''Of course, you should have gone. You still a tea drinker?''

Sniffing, she nodded.

He put water on to boil. ''Don't feel guilty,'' Harrison said firmly. ''You needed the time to be responsible only for yourself. As I've discovered this past week, it's exhausting to constantly care for children.''

''You had an unusual week.''

''True, and I admit to looking forward to being alone again.''

Stephanie still looked miserable.

''Okay, will it make you feel any better if I admit to actually looking up the telephone number of a helicopter chartering company so I could find you and bring you home?''

That earned a smile, as he'd expected.

"What did I tell you? Raising kids is hard."

Harrison smiled ruefully. "You were right. I can't remember, did we have a bet?"

"Hearing you admit that I was right is payment enough for me."

Harrison poured boiling water into a cup, dunked in a tea bag and sat on the bar stool next to her. "So tell me about your great wilderness adventure."

"Why, Harrison. You've gone all domestic."

"It'll wear off."

Stephanie laughed.

They spent twenty minutes talking, something Harrison couldn't ever remember doing with his sister-in-law. He was in the middle of telling her what had happened with the board when he heard a quiet knock.

"I'll bet that's Carrie." Harrison started for the door. "I want you to meet her."

It was Carrie, and one look at her face told him that she'd already heard about the board meeting.

"We'll talk later," he murmured. "Stephanie is here to get Nathan and Matthew."

Carrie nodded tightly. "I'm glad I'll get to say goodbye."

Harrison introduced the two women, curious to see how they'd get along.

Stephanie was predisposed to like any woman who had cared for her children while they'd been sick and Carrie was a subdued version of her bubbly self, which had the effect of making her appear solid and reliable.

All in all, Harrison thought, it was an auspicious first meeting and first impressions were important.

Stephanie went to wake up Nathan and get him ready to go. Any reservations she might have had about Carrie obviously fled when Nathan saw her. "Cawee," he said, and pointed.

"Yes, that's Carrie," Stephanie said.

"Nathan, you want to give me a bye-bye hug?" Carrie asked, and opened her arms. Nathan went running to her, and she hugged him fiercely.

Harrison mentally stepped up the timetable for having children. Carrie was obviously ready. The fact that he hadn't mentioned his vision of their future to Carrie didn't bother him at all. It was all part of his plan and above all, Harrison excelled at plans.

At last all the baby equipment and supplies were loaded into Stephanie's van and they were gone.

Harrison had barely shut the door when Carrie burst out, "What *happened* at the board meeting?"

"They voted against you. I'm sorry." Taking her hand, Harrison led her to the sofa, which he moved back into position. "And I can't even say I did my best." He told her pretty much everything, including Nathan's artwork on the tables.

Incredibly Carrie laughed. "I wish I could have been there, especially when they cited you!"

"It wasn't my finest hour."

"Oh, Harry, I can just see you, all flustered and disorganized, telling off that snobby woman. I know how you like to have everything all orderly and arranged in a certain way, but even though you weren't ready, you gave it your best shot."

"Unfortunately I was using a slingshot when I should have had an elephant gun."

Carrie stared off into space. "Now that you mention it, Mrs. Greenborough does look like an elephant.''

"I'll be ready for her next time. I filed an appeal for you, and I've already got a plan in place. I'm going to have my lawyer take a look at the Residents' Agreement. Then, we're going to spend the next month patrolling this place and filing complaints on every single violation we find. The—''

"Harrison, it's not worth it.''

"But you'll have to move." Carrie moving wasn't in his plans.

"They'll make my life even more miserable than it already is. Anyway, I'm going to quit my job, so it doesn't matter if I live someplace else.'' She almost sounded convincing.

"It matters to me," Harrison told her firmly.

"It does?'' She turned her face to his.

He looked at her, trying to imagine not ever seeing Carrie again. "It does very much," he whispered.

Now wasn't this the perfect moment for a kiss? Harrison thought so, and also figured that when the reality of getting kicked out of her home sank in, he wouldn't get another opportunity until Carrie got over being mad at him.

However, kissing her wasn't on the schedule until they'd had a formal date. Harrison hadn't had any luck lately when he deviated from his plans and schedules. Kissing her now might not be a good idea.

Carrie's eyes grew wide and her lips parted. She looked great. Her hair was loose and she wore what he thought of as her folk singer look—long flimsy skirt and a tiny T-shirt in a soft fabric. A touchable fabric. In fact, Carrie was looking generally touchable. She was all curls and curves, her softness and smiles made even more alluring by the fact that he knew they hid strength.

Harrison decided to expand the definition of what constituted a date. They were together. That was good enough for him.

He lowered his mouth to hers.

She tasted of sweet promise and shared goals. Her kiss was at once familiar and new, and as potent as before.

This time, he was prepared. Burying his hands in her curls, he angled his mouth over hers, seeking the perfect fit he remembered.

Once he found it, he stopped thinking and surrendered to the feelings. His last conscious thought was that a total surrender at this stage probably wasn't a wise idea, but by then it was too late.

Kissing Carrie was like jumping off the high dive. You were either thinking about diving, or you were falling toward the water. No in between.

And so, he dived right in.

He felt Carrie's hands on his shoulders and lifted his mouth.

"Harrison, what are we doing?" Her voice was breathy.

"I'm kissing you. I want to kiss you." He nuzzled her neck. "Lots." He nipped her earlobe. Carrie made a little humming sound. "For hours and hours."

She still hadn't allowed him to kiss her mouth again. For the moment, he was content to explore the sensitive nerve endings of her neck. For the moment. "I want to kiss you until your taste and scent is imprinted on my memory and I can recall them at will."

"Ooh, that's a good line."

"Thanks. It's not a line. It's the truth."

"Is it? Because I hope it is and I don't want to get hurt."

He pulled back and gazed at her. Her eyes were wide and vulnerable. His heart filled. "I won't hurt you. It's too early to put a name to what we feel for each other, but it's real and it's there and I intend to let it grow."

"Then I'll put a name to it—love."

Harrison brushed her hair off her forehead. "Waiting to see if I'll bolt?"

"Yes."

He smiled, his lips still warm from her skin. "I'm still here."

"So now what?"

Gathering her closer, he said, "This works for me."

"Oh, Harrison..." She sighed. "Don't you want me to kiss you?"

"Very much."

"Well, then, give me a chance."

Oh.

Carrie's arms curled around him and she brought her lips to his in a gentle fusing that soon turned torrid.

Her tongue touched his and he felt the warmth all the way to his toes.

He pressed her back against the couch—he must have for he became aware that more of him was touching Carrie than before and this was a good thing.

He skimmed his hand up her rib cage and felt her hands on his back, then individual sensations all melted together as they explored each other.

Time stopped for Harrison, something that rarely happened.

Neither of them heard the perfunctory knock and the jangle of keys.

But they did hear the scream.

They broke apart so fast, Harrison was dizzy, and blinked as he tried to get his bearings. Beside him, Carrie adjusted her clothes and hair.

Mrs. Petrovich, his maid, stood in the doorway, clutching cleaning supplies to her ample bodice. *"Mester Rrrrothwelll!"* Sagging against the doorway, she muttered in her native tongue. "You gave me such a fright. What you do here in the middle of the day? And with a young lady." She clicked her tongue. "You want I should come back?"

"No, no," Harrison hastened to reassure her. "My nephews visited this week and the place desperately needs your touch."

He reached for Carrie's hand to find her charmingly flustered. "This is Carrie who lives downstairs."

"Hello Carrie-who-lives-downstairs."

"I'd planned to ask Mrs. Petrovich for input on a chapter dealing with housecleaning rules for the *Domestic Primer*," Harrison said, more to fill the silence than anything. But, it was a brilliant idea, if he said so himself.

"Rules, shmools," Mrs. Petrovich said as she ruthlessly marched around the room straightening with a precision that Harrison admired. "If it's clean, it works, if it isn't, it's dirty."

"What did she say?" Carrie asked, speaking for the first time.

"I'm not sure, but it sounded profound," Harrison answered. "Mrs. Petrovich, we're going for coffee to get out of your way."

"Good. Shoo!"

They closed the door, silently walked to the stairwell, took one look at each other and burst into laughter. Harrison took her hand. "Sorry about that. I forgot about Mrs. Petrovich coming this afternoon."

"It's just as well."

Privately Harrison agreed and was glad Carrie understood. They were building a future here. They needed to establish a solid foundation first. "My car is at this end." Harrison gestured.

"We don't have to leave," Carrie said as they walked down the stairs. She smiled up at him with an irresistible shyness. "My place is just on the corner."

"Sounds good." Harrison was eager to see this place that had been the cause of friction between Carrie and the condo board for untold months.

He anticipated an eclectic style with whimsical folk art and pottery. Carrie looked like a pottery person. Maybe stained glass, as well.

He hoped her couch was comfortable.

Throwing a tentative smile over her shoulder, Carrie unlocked her door.

Harrison stepped inside after her, stopped and grabbed her arm.

The place looked as if it had been bombed, or at the very least ransacked. Even now, the intruder might still be there.

He pulled Carrie to him protectively.

"What?" She laughed as she stumbled back and landed in his arms.

Belatedly Harrison registered the fact that she had neither screamed, nor recoiled in dismay at the sight of her studio apartment.

This must be the way it normally looked.

Hair everywhere on his body stood on end. His stomach clenched at the sight of the chaos.

Carrie was still waiting for him to explain why he'd grabbed her. "I just wanted you near me," he murmured, surprised he could actually speak.

"That's so sweet." She sighed and covered his arms with hers. They stood swaying slightly—Carrie no doubt finding the situation romantic.

Harrison was merely trying to keep his balance against the assault on his sense of order.

"Well, this is it. Home sweet home. What do you think?"

"It's smaller than I thought." *Especially with all the clutter.*

The room was longer than it was wide—literally a leftover slice from the renovations. It reminded him of a boxcar.

Carrie drew him inside. Walking over to a couch upholstered in a plaid no sane Scotsman had ever worn, she swept newspapers, magazines, mail, advertising flyers, catalogs, computer printouts, a diskette and an empty candy bar wrapper into one pile, which she patted until she could pick it all up at once, then dumped it on the floor beside sofa. "I suppose I let things get a little messy this week."

"You've been busy," Harrison managed to say. And actually, she had. He knew from the way she left his home when she'd been watching the boys that she was capable of picking things up.

But, his house was basically in order. She only had to use it like a guide.

Harrison felt marginally better. In the past, he'd gone into companies in such disarray that he wondered how they could function. The solutions that seemed so apparent to him were beyond the executive personnel, but once Harrison had shown them how to organize and streamline, they'd been able to maintain his principles of time management on their own.

That's all he needed to do here. She'd be grateful. Most people were. He smiled at Carrie, who had been watching him anxiously. "You mentioned coffee?"

"Oh, coffee!" She laughed and gestured with her hands. "I forgot...over here."

Her kitchen consisted of a two-burner stove, oven, a microwave that took up all the counterspace next to the sink and a refrigerator that dominated the area, though it was much smaller than his. Magnets holding menus, notes and postcards covered every square inch of the surface.

Two wrought-iron chairs with red-and-white striped plastic seats were next to a tiny matching table. Carrie removed the clothing draped over them and invited Harrison to sit. He did, tilting because the chair he selected had one leg shorter than the other.

Carrie filled a kettle and put it on to boil, then opened a cabinet filled with jars, bottles, cans and cereal boxes all obviously shoved in at random. She had to take out and replace several items before finding the coffee.

A jar of instant.

She doesn't have room for a coffeemaker, Harrison lectured himself, though, personally, he'd always find room for a coffeemaker.

Their conversation had been nonexistent since they'd arrived and Harrison was afraid Carrie had sensed his disapproval. He didn't want to hurt her feelings, but how could she live like this?

"We need to discuss a couple of things," he stated, without his usual finesse.

"I can tell that something is bothering you," Carrie said. She opened the other cabinet and Harrison winced at her dishes. They were all different colors, though of the same pattern. She got out a pink mug and a turquoise one.

Harrison hoped she gave him the turquoise. "I believe you should fight the eviction."

"They'll just outvote you again."

"Maybe, but I want to make it uncomfortable for them."

She leaned against the refrigerator and crossed her arms. "What's the point?"

"The point is that they're wrong."

"You talk as though you're not a part of them."

He hadn't felt like a part of the board since the meeting. "I'm going to resign from the board if they vote to evict you."

"Technically I *did* violate the rules they cited me for."

"And I've wondered why. After the first few citations, you had to have known how picky they were."

"Honestly, I never decided to break any of their silly rules. But maybe subconsciously I wanted to be forced to leave."

"I don't understand." And he wanted to.

"When I first moved in, it was right after I left school and my dad found this place. He and my mother decided it was where my friend and I should live. You know, respectable, a good location. And it was—is. But it's also staid and old-fashioned."

Harrison found it tasteful and serene. He glanced

around Carrie's living room again and could see why she felt stifled by the rules.

"We wanted a party complex catering to singles. The thing was, if we agreed to live here, our parents would kick in half the rent, but give us nothing if we picked a different place."

She hadn't done anything thousands in her position hadn't done before. "Under the circumstances, it sounds like you made a smart decision to me."

"It's just...it's like where I live is the only thing that I've done that's pleased my parents. They tell everyone they know that I live here. It impresses people. 'She must be doing very well for herself' they say. It makes up for the fact that I haven't settled on a career."

"I get the idea. But don't you think getting evicted will upset your parents?"

"Everything I do upsets my parents."

"Then why—"

"Look. I messed up, okay? I forgot about the planters and the recycling and all the other stuff. I didn't do any of it on purpose, but what do these people do, sit around all day and memorize the Residents' Agreement? I don't even know where mine is."

Harrison was not at all surprised. "Carrie, let me help you." He was referring to getting her organized, as well as tackling the board.

She shook her head. "If they don't get me this time, they'll keep trying until they do. Don't you get crosswise with them over it. Once I'm gone, they'll be looking for a new target."

She was undoubtedly correct, but Harrison was going to fight, anyway.

The water boiled and Carrie spooned powdered coffee into the mugs. She added the water, stirred briefly and brought the mugs over to the table. She set one in front of him. The pink one.

Harrison stared at his coffee. Tiny flecks of undissolved powder clung to the yellow foam.

"You take it black, right?"

"Yes, black is fine." He leaned forward, putting his elbows on the tiny round table, then removing them, when it, too, tilted. "I did want to talk with you about something else. Somehow," he gave her a look, "Felicia believes that you are my assistant on the *Domestic Primer* project."

Carrie grinned. "It seemed expedient at the time."

"I wondered if you'd like to make it official."

"What do you mean?"

"I'm offering to hire you. Part-time, or, if you decide to stop reviewing bands and clubs, full-time."

"Really?" She looked so pleased, that Harrison was glad he'd come up with the idea. "What would I do?"

"I'll develop a survey, and you'll interview people, handle all correspondence, transcribe notes and whatever else needs to be done. Probably talk to Felicia on the phone a lot."

"Hey, I like that idea. It doesn't have a forever feel to it, but it'll make a good transition job." She picked up her coffee. "My parents will love it."

"Part-time, or full-time? Your call."

"Full-time," she admitted with a sheepish smile. "You know how I said I was going to quit my job? Well, actually, I wrote up a week's worth of reviews and sent them with my letter of resignation this morning."

Mentally Harrison did a victory dance, outwardly

he said, "Great", then picked up his mug and sipped at the nasty stuff masquerading as coffee.

"Where will I work?"

Harrison hadn't got that far, not anticipating that Carrie would have already given up her night job. "With me at the Rothwell building. We'll set up a spot for you somewhere." Even if it had to be in a corner of his office.

This was going better than he'd dreamed. With Carrie working for him, she'd be sure to absorb the Rothwell tenets. And, she'd be testing the theories of the *Domestic Primer*, at the same time.

In twenty-one days, the usual length of time of a full Rothwell training session, Carrie Brent would be living the Rothwell way and wondering how she'd ever existed before.

CHAPTER TEN

"SHARON, you remember Carrie Brent?"

Harrison's secretary eyed Carrie. "Oh, yes."

Carrie had made an effort today, her first day. Harrison knew she was going for the hard-edged career woman look by wearing a severely tailored navy blue suit and pulling her curls into a bumpy bun. He liked the suit, but wished she'd let down her hair.

"Carrie's going to be working here with us," he said.

"Of course she is."

Harrison gave Sharon an if-you-want-to-get-promoted-change-your-attitude-quick look.

Sharon brightened her expression. "Wonderful news."

Too bright.

"I'm sure we'll get along like a house afire," Carrie said. Her smile was too bright as well.

Harrison cleared his throat. "Carrie's assisting me on the Domestic Primer project. She's already met with Felicia." What a stretch. "And helped me with the boys last week. All calls concerning the Primer should route through Carrie and she'll report directly to me. Any questions?"

Carrie spoke up. "Where's my desk?"

"Cubicle D. Sharon will show you. Also, Sharon, will you program the telephones and show Carrie how to work her voice mail? And send e-mail out about her location and phone number. I'll introduce her to everyone at the staff meeting."

"Hi, Carrie. Welcome to Rothwell." Jon stopped by Sharon's desk to hand her some papers, then approached them. "I understand you were quite a help with my sons last week. I want to thank you."

Carrie's face lit up. "No—I enjoyed it, really. In fact, I miss them."

"Well, I'd bring them to visit, but you know that place of yours." He raised his eyebrows.

Harrison wished he hadn't told Jon about the citation since his brother hadn't stopped kidding him about it. He'd also found the details of Felicia's visit hilarious, though Harrison had rebuked him for not keeping him informed.

"I would like to see the boys again," Carrie said wistfully, completely missing Jon's sarcasm.

"Harrison, you'll have to bring her out for a visit." Jon winked at him, thinking he was teasing Harrison. Little did he know that a lot had changed in the week he'd been away.

"How about next weekend?" Harrison countered.

After a surprised look, Jon recovered nicely. "Let me get with Stephanie and I'll let you know times and such." He patted his brother on the arm, nodded to Carrie and retreated to his office.

The little byplay hadn't been lost on Sharon, who now regarded Carrie with more respect.

Harrison was glad he wouldn't have any more trouble there. "I'll leave you with Sharon." He smiled encouragingly at Carrie. "Give me a call if you need anything."

Then he strode into his office. It was good to be back.

* * *

By afternoon, Carrie's hair was out of its bun. By three o'clock, she'd become so comfortable in the office that she left her shoes under her desk and walked the hallway in stocking feet.

But by Thursday, Harrison realized things had progressed from overfamiliarity to All Was Not Well.

He arrived at his usual time. Sharon was not at her desk. Come to think of it few people had been at their desks when he'd walked by. Curious, he approached Carrie's cubicle. She wasn't there, either, but it was obvious that she had been.

Incredibly Carrie's cubicle resembled her cluttered home. Papers were tacked all over the cubicle walls. Yes, the material was made to accommodate tacks and staples, but Harrison strongly discouraged tacking papers. He encouraged filing papers.

Carrie's file drawer was empty, except for an umbrella, a package of panty hose and an apple.

Papers, office supplies and sticky notes littered every surface including the telephone handset. Tiny plastic toys—the kind that came with fast-food meals—perched on top of her computer monitor. A gargoyle sat on the divider between her cubicle and the next. Beside it sat a gargoyle facing the opposite direction. Harrison walked to the next cubicle, not liking what he saw. Comics and fortunes from fortune cookies littered the walls.

Up and down the aisles, he walked, noting that Carrie's influence had spread. Rather than Carrie absorbing *Rothwell's Rules*, Rothwell employees were absorbing Carrie's Clutter.

And where was everyone?

He heard laughter coming from the coffee lounge

and discovered the majority of his staff crowded into the room.

"Hi, Harry!"

Snickers followed Carrie's greeting, since everyone knew how he hated to be called Harry. Why didn't she remember?

"I made my special oatmeal/wheat-germ/bran muffins. Nobody around here gets enough fiber. I used dried cranberries instead of raisins. Want one?"

No, he didn't want one. He wanted to yell at everyone to get back to work. One look at their faces told him that's what they were expecting.

One look at Carrie's eager-to-please face told him that public criticism would devastate her.

"Sure. I'll have a muffin." He took a bite. "Good." Nodding around the room, he said mildly, "Back to work everybody."

In a remarkably short time, he and Carrie were alone in the lounge. Setting the remainder of his muffin on a napkin, he dusted his fingertips.

"Don't you like it?"

"Yes, it tastes good, but I ate breakfast at 6:42 this morning."

Carrie's smile faded. "Well, this is a snack."

"The Rothwell workday begins promptly at eight o'clock. Any snacking should be done prior to that time."

Carrie twisted the giant watch she wore so the face was toward her. "It's only ten past."

"It is thirteen minutes past eight. That's thirteen minutes lost from each employee who was in here. Including you, I counted a dozen. That's thirteen minutes times twelve people, or one hundred fifty-six minutes of lost productivity. That's over two and a half hours.''

Carrie slammed the muffin plate on the counter. ''Well, excuse me, Mr. Scrooge!'' She flounced toward her desk.

He wasn't finished with the discussion, but it would be better to continue it when they'd both cooled down.

Avoiding going by Carrie's cubicle on the way back, Harrison returned to his office—now behind schedule, himself, and signaled Sharon to bring him the various notes and messages she'd collected since yesterday.

During the first hour of the workday, Harrison dealt with returning phone calls, or better yet, leaving messages on voice mail, and small tasks that took less than five minutes. By lumping them together in a block of time, he kept them from piling up, or taking more time than was warranted. It was a Rothwell Rule.

Sharon walked into his office. She was not wearing shoes.

Carrie's influence had taken root faster than he'd thought. Harrison could hardly force himself to concentrate on what Sharon was telling him.

How had one employee had such a great—and horrible—influence in such a short time?

What was going on?

Pushing the folder Sharon had brought him aside, Harrison opened his file drawer and withdrew his company analysis forms.

He was going to objectively analyze this situation as though he were analyzing any other company.

Twenty-three minutes later, he was no closer to the

solution, so he knocked on the connecting door to Jon's office.

"Come in!" Jon called.

When Harrison entered, he saw Jon was on the phone. Even worse, he was talking to Stephanie. It was a personal call on company time.

Even Jon was forgetting the tenets of the Rothwell philosophy.

"What's up?" he asked cheerfully as he hung up the phone.

"Maybe you can tell me." Instead of sitting, Harrison paced. "I arrived to find everybody having a party in the employee coffee room. In addition, their work areas are trashed. And nobody is wearing shoes anymore!"

"Carrie's influence."

"I *know!* What I don't know is why, or how." Harrison showed his brother the analysis he'd done of the situation.

Jon laughed. "There's no mystery. You give Carrie preferential treatment. Everybody's noticed."

"I do not."

"No? A couple of weeks ago, she showed up here, threw a tantrum and got in to see you. Now, she's working here as your personal assistant on a project that will make a huge impact on the company."

Harrison shoved his hands into his pockets. "That just sort of happened. And it's only temporary."

"Nobody knows that. And didn't it occur to you that there are several people who should have been considered for the promotion?"

"It's not a promotion."

"Hello? She's an executive assistant!"

The same title Sharon had asked for. He'd better

give it to her immediately. "That—that's Felicia's doing. Carrie's actually more a project assistant."

Jon shook his head. "If it walks like a duck and talks like a duck...you get the idea. She reports directly to you. She answers to nobody else. She does whatever she wants and isn't reprimanded—people notice these things, Hare."

Jon was right. Harrison sank into the chair and covered his eyes. His employees resented her and this was the way they were letting him know. "What should I do?"

"You should get rid of her, but you won't because you're in love with her."

In love with Carrie. He didn't bother to deny it, not even to himself. His love was ahead of schedule, but it was there, nevertheless. "Does everyone know?"

"Probably. But they like Carrie." Jon smiled. "Stephanie and I do, too."

Harrison exhaled. All his frustrations during the week came pouring out. "I don't know why I love her. She's completely disorganized. I knew this, yet when she was watching the boys, she was incredibly efficient. I thought it was a matter of education. I thought seeing the Rothwell philosophy in action would help her. I thought she'd *want* to learn."

"Poor Hare." But Jon looked amused, not sympathetic.

"So where's the efficiency?" Harrison shook his head. "She's misplaced papers, she's constantly phoned to asked questions, she's failed to complete reports in a timely manner—not that I knew what she was working on because she never got around to doing her daily status reports. Rather than trying to keep to a schedule, she is spending all her time revising her schedule. Or decorating her cubicle!"

"Why do you demand daily progress reports from Carrie and weekly ones from everyone else?"

"I thought it would help teach her organizational skills—and so I know what she's doing!"

"She's doing her job, Harrison. She's doing it very well. You wonder why she's had such an influence. It's because she's been interviewing our staff about their home life—just the way you asked her to. Yes, her methods are unorthodox, but she's getting information we never would have. People like her, so they talk to her."

Narrowing his eyes, Harrison asked, "How do you know this?"

"I've seen her, and I've heard it from Felicia."

"You've talked with Felicia?"

Jon leveled a look at him. "Hare, you are developing a tendency to micromanage. That's not efficient."

Harrison hated it when his brother was right. "Neither is Carrie," he grumbled.

"She may not be working the way you want her to, but she is making progress on gathering data for the primer."

"I'll have to take your word for it," Harrison said dryly.

Jon came out from behind his desk. "Many couples can't work together. I probably couldn't work with Stephanie."

"It's worse than that. I don't think I can *live* with her. You ought to see her apartment. It's worse than her cubicle."

Jon stared down at him. "I hadn't realized things had progressed so far between you."

"They haven't, but the issue will have to be faced."

"Have you told her how you feel?"

"No."

"What? You expect her to read your mind?"

No, but couldn't she see the way he lived? Hadn't she read the Rothwell employee's manual? "I'll talk to her," Harrison said.

Harrison went back to his abbreviated morning routine before calling Carrie into his office.

She came bubbling in, smiling and lighting up the place. Apparently she'd forgiven him for his reprimand this morning.

Disregarding his instructions about ignoring their personal relationship during business hours, Carrie threw her arms around his neck and kissed him.

"Oh, Harrison, I'm sorry I got mad. I hate feeling angry with you. I just didn't think a few minutes were that big of a deal, but I can see they are to you and after all, this *is* your company, so I'll try to remember and do better."

Harrison felt like a louse.

She kissed him again, until he murmured a protest.

Laughing, she drew back. "What's wrong? I shut the door."

"You make it difficult for me to concentrate." He sat, deliberately putting his desk between them.

She grinned, obviously pleased with herself. "Listen, I've got the best news about the primer. Doug— he's in the cubicle next to mine—Doug showed me how to get on the Internet! Of course I've heard people talk about it, but I thought it was for techno geeks, you know?''

She paused only long enough for him to nod. ''Well, there is just tons of information on that thing. I can post my survey and get responses from all over the world! That's what I wanted to see you about. I thought I'd better ask you first.''

''You thought right.''

She frowned at his tone. ''Don't you think it's a good idea?''

''It could be,'' he said, trying not to further dampen her enthusiasm. ''But I'd want the lawyers to take a look first. Have a seat.''

''Okay.'' She sat in a chair and looked at him expectantly.

This next part was going to be hard. ''I need to talk with you about a couple of things. Have you had a chance to read your employee handbook yet?''

She stared at her hands. ''Not all the way through.''

Not any of the way through, he suspected. ''You need to do so. You see, my company is in the business of teaching other companies more efficient ways to conduct their business.''

''I know that.''

''I can't very well sell efficiency ideas to a company if my own company isn't practicing them. That's why I insist that my employees follow *Rothwell's Rules of Time Management.*''

''I've been reading about some of that in your book.''

She'd been reading his book and still... ''You need to follow the rules, too, Carrie.''

She threw up her hands. ''Who can remember them all?''

"The thousands of people who've attended my seminars have had no difficulty."

"They just haven't told you."

He couldn't believe he had to argue with her about this. "Carrie, the basic rules are in the employee handbook. Please familiarize yourself with it. Start with the chapter on maintaining your work space. I discourage tacking up junky papers and clippings and displaying knickknacks. Clutter causes inefficiency."

"Not for me."

He'd let that pass for now. "I can't let you ignore company policy while insisting the other employees follow it."

"Even if it's a stupid policy?"

"Especially if it's a stupid policy."

A smile teased the corners of her mouth and he knew she wasn't taking him seriously. "Please clean up your desk and remove the toys and cartoons. I'm sending a memo out to that effect immediately."

"Lighten up, Harry. I'll go clean my space and turn myself into a drone like the rest of your employees." She stood.

"I don't want you to be a drone."

"Well, have you ever considered that the most efficient way might not be the best way? People are only human. You've got to consider that."

He smiled at the typical Carrie philosophy. "I have, believe it or not. Which is the other thing I wanted to discuss with you. Spending the week with Matthew and Nathan made me realize I'd underestimated the impact children had on an employee's life. Worrying about child care, in particular, is bound to affect a worker's job performance. I'm thinking of establish-

ing an emergency child care center here. I don't think
we can offer full-time care, but surely we can—''

"Oh, Harrison!" Carrie ran over, sat in his lap and
hugged him. "It's perfect! Doing the survey, I heard
about child care problems over and over again. You'll
see it in my notes—I knew there was a reason I fell
in love with you!"

"Does this mean you want to research this project,
too?"

"Could I?"

Harrison nodded, feeling relieved. Carrie would
come around. Things would work out.

Things were not working out.

By the end of the following week, Harrison suggested that Carrie could work from her home, since
she was spending most of her time visiting day care
centers. She agreed, with visible relief.

She was trying to follow Rothwell's Rules, he knew
she was, but her inability to do so was affecting their
personal relationship.

The third time he had to wait on her because she
couldn't find a shoe, or her purse, or something else
she'd lost in the organizational disaster in which she
lived, he came to a decision.

"Carrie?"

"I saw the coupon right here yesterday." She
pawed through a pile of papers.

"It's okay. Forget it."

"But I don't want you to pay full price when I've
got a coupon."

"I can afford it." He didn't like fried fish all that
much anyway.

"Just because you can afford it doesn't mean you

should pay full price—here it is.'' Triumphantly she withdrew a grocery store receipt. ''The coupon is on the back.''

''Good. Carrie?''

''What?'' She was stuffing the receipt into her purse, which she'd had to search for earlier.

''We need to get this place organized.''

She eyed him suspiciously. ''Why?''

''Well, you need a place to work and file your papers.''

She pointed to her coffee table in front of the sofa. ''That's where I work.''

''There's also the possibility that you'll have to move in a few weeks, if the board denies your appeal.'' He hadn't wanted to bring that up. ''You'd have to go through your stuff then, anyway.''

''Couldn't I just move it all?'' The distressed expression on her face told him he was dealing with the worst sort of packrat.

The situation required finesse. ''We've been working together on a household management system. I need to test it.'' He gestured around. ''What better place? We can do it this weekend. In fact, after dinner, we can go shopping for containers and organizers. It'll be fun.''

As it turned out, Saturday was not fun. Carrie questioned every item Harrison discarded until he felt he'd go crazy with frustration. Fortunately she'd planned to tour a day care center while it was closed for the weekend. Harrison suggested she take the director to lunch, his treat.

While Carrie was gone, he engaged in a wholesale clearing out as fast as he could. He culled the paper piles for bills and tossed the rest. He went through her drawers and her cabinets, but left her clothes alone. He would have liked to have burned her furniture, too. There was no way any of it was going to end up in his tastefully decorated condo.

He hadn't mentioned marriage to Carrie yet, but when she adjusted to this new way of living, he knew he would. Smiling, he dumped a particularly ugly and battered cooking pot. Their marriage would be her reward for living the organized life.

"Where's all my stuff?" Carrie demanded. She opened a drawer, gasped, then opened another and gasped again.

Harrison had been prepared for fervent expressions of gratitude. He'd been prepared for her to twirl around, arms outspread, reveling in all the space.

And, yes, he'd been prepared for a few objections.

"What have you done?" Carrie was in her tiny kitchen, the cabinet doors wide-open.

"I threw out any cracked or chipped dishes and a couple of hideous cooking pots. Oh, and about a thousand wire twist ties. I think they breed in the drawer."

"What am I supposed to use for dishes when my friends come over?"

She served her friends on chipped dishes?

"And the pot—that was my gumbo pot. It holds exactly the right amount of gumbo to feed everybody."

"Couldn't you buy another one?"

"Why should I? I had a perfectly fine gumbo pot."

"It was...ugly."

"It had charm and character and had simmered gallons of gumbo."

Carrie left the cabinets open as she went storming into her living area. Harrison closed the doors.

Carrie looked under her sofa and chair, then yanked back the curtain blocking her bed from the room and looked under it, too. "Where are the newspapers?"

Harrison was losing his patience. "That stack in the corner was months old! If you haven't read them by now, you're not going to."

"You threw away the newspapers?" Her voice held the beginnings of panic.

"Yes, of course I did." And he wasn't going to apologize, either.

"*Those were my reviews.* They were the only copies I had!"

"Why didn't you cut out your reviews and file them?"

"I was going to," she said defensively.

"No, you weren't. You were going to keep stacking the papers until they reached the ceiling."

Carrie glared at him and headed for the door.

"Where are you going?"

"To the trash."

"Carrie—you can get copies from the newspaper—Carrie, wait!"

"Tell me," she snapped, when he caught up with her. "Do I have any clothes left to wear, or did you throw away everything that didn't meet with your approval?"

"I didn't touch your clothes or your makeup, but why you need seventeen tubes of lipstick is beyond me. I left your bathroom stuff alone—except for getting rid of the outdated medicine and the empty prescription bottles."

"Ooh! That's how I keep track of the medicine I've taken so I know what works."

Her reasoning was beyond him. "Carrie, the doctor and the pharmacy will have it on file."

They reached back of the complex where two giant trash Dumpsters sat.

"Where's my stuff?"

He pointed to the nearest one.

Carrie ran over and looked inside. "I see my pot!" She gripped the edge. "Help me climb up."

"You're *not* climbing into the Dumpster to pick through God knows what."

"Fine, I'll do it myself." To Harrison's horror, she hoisted herself up the side, swung her leg over and dropped inside the Dumpster.

"Carrie—" He had to dodge a flying gumbo pot. "Carrie?"

"What?" She heaved a box over the side.

"Think about what you're doing."

"I know exactly what I'm doing. I'm getting my stuff back."

Harrison couldn't bear the thought of her rummaging through everyone's trash. Knowing her, she'd come back with more than he'd thrown out. "Carrie, listen to me."

She wouldn't, so Harrison climbed inside the Dumpster and gripped her shoulders.

She was crying. "My stuff. You threw it all away."

"Oh, Carrie." He hugged her to him. "I know it must hurt, but you'll never miss most of it. We've got your gumbo pot back. Why don't you just leave the rest?"

Pushing away from him, she bent and dug through the trash. "Oh, no!" Standing, she thrust a plastic

Batman figure into his face. "You threw out my fast-food toy collection, didn't you?"

Harrison remembered them lining the window sills and shelves. "Yes."

Carrie pointed. "Start digging. I had a hundred and three and I want every one of them back."

"They...they won't fit in with my decor."

"What?" She shoved her hair out of her eyes.

This wasn't the time, and it certainly wasn't the place, but unless Harrison explained, he was going to spend the next hour in a trash Dumpster.

"I said, they won't fit in with my decor." He took her hand. "Carrie, you must know how I feel about you. I want you to be a part of my life. I'm talking marriage and children here. But I can't stand disorganization and clutter. I can't. And I couldn't let you move that mess into my house."

Several different emotions had flickered across her face. Undiluted joy was not one of them. "I don't recall being asked."

"I'm not going to propose in a trash Dumpster, but it is my plan to ask you to marry me some time in the near future."

"What are you waiting for?"

"I'm waiting until we're both sure. This is a life-time commitment. It will be a big change for you."

She blinked. "And not for you?"

Harrison was conscious that he hadn't expressed himself well. "I want you to get used to your new way of life before adding marriage to the mix."

"*My* new way of life?"

"Yes. I don't expect you to become organized and efficient all at once. You'll have to work at it."

She stared at him. "Work at it?"

"Why are you repeating everything I say?"

"Because I don't believe what you're saying! You want *me* to fit into *your* life, do things *your* way, move into *your* house—in other words, completely change myself."

Harrison looked at it as improving. "Don't you want to change?"

Stepping back, she shook her head. "No, Harrison, I don't. If you love me, then you'll have to accept me the way I am."

CHAPTER ELEVEN

Two weeks had passed since Harrison had stood in a trash Dumpster and picked out Carrie's "stuff."

They'd both agreed that they had no future together. It was all very civil and organized. Carrie neatly severed all connection with him, and turned over her papers and files in excruciating order.

She was becoming organized in spite of herself. She just didn't realize it.

In Harrison's office, cartoons, fortunes and gargoyles disappeared from the cubicles and people wore shoes once more.

Sharon was promoted to executive assistant.

And no one smiled.

Least of all Harrison.

After work each day, he returned home to his pristine condo—his empty, pristine condo—his lonely, empty, pristine condo. He tried to work on the *Domestic Primer*, but felt as if he were a fraud. Even sleeping all the way through the night didn't make him feel better.

The truth was, he'd broken all the Rothwell's Rules that week he'd spent with his nephews. Children did not follow those sorts of rules. They followed Carrie's kind of rules, but the problem was that Carrie seemed to make the rules up as she went along.

Even imposing *Rothwell's Rules* at work made him feel like a hypocrite. He hadn't been able to follow them at all once he had children like the majority of his employees.

He was efficient, but apparently not realistic.

He read over Carrie's surveys and was appalled at the struggle some of his employees engaged in daily. Yes, there needed to be a primer, but increasingly, Harrison didn't feel he was the one to write it—at least not alone.

He needed Carrie—but not the chaos that was her life.

Knowing he was inflicting himself on his brother, but too dejected to care, Harrison invited himself over for Sunday dinner. As a peace offering, he picked up a gourmet apple pie from Stephanie's favorite bakery. Once he got there, he impulsively bought a peach one, as well.

Driving out to the suburbs, Harrison berated himself for the fact that his impulses extended only to buying too much dessert.

He was in the kitchen unwrapping the pies when he saw Nathan.

"Hawee!" Nathan ran toward him, arms outstretched.

"Hey, Nathan!" Harrison scooped him up and hugged him so tightly, the little boy squirmed. Harrison relaxed his grip, surprised that he missed Nathan so much.

"Cawee?" Nathan looked around.

"Carrie's not…Carrie's not here," Harrison managed to say.

"Why?"

"That's his new word," Stephanie said. "Better get used to it."

Harrison hoped that was Nathan's only new word.

After lunch, Matthew and Nathan went down for their naps. Stephanie returned to the room, refilled Harrison's coffee, then sat down and fixed him with a stern look. "Okay, spill. What happened between you and Carrie?"

Harrison looked at Jon. "I thought you told her."

"I did. She didn't believe me."

"You could not be that stupid," Stephanie said. "So what really happened?"

Harrison told her, adding the part about mentioning marriage to Carrie.

Stephanie's mouth fell open. "You proposed to her in a trash Dumpster after you threw away all her things?"

"I didn't formally propose, but I told her I wanted her to be a part of my life."

"What about being a part of her life?"

"But her life is...is chaotic. Who'd want to live that way?"

Stephanie looked at Jon. "I apologize. He *is* that stupid."

"I can't live the way she does," Harrison insisted.

Stephanie looked at him as she drank her coffee. "Jon tells me that things are back to normal at the office. Home, too, I guess?"

"Yes."

"All tidy and arranged just the way you want it?"

"Yes."

"And are you happy?"

No, he wasn't happy, and it was all Carrie's fault. Where before he found serenity, now he found blandness. His drawers and shelves looked barren, not neat. The office was sterile.

"I'm guessing you feel pretty miserable, right?"

Harrison nodded. "But I'd be miserable surrounded by all her junk, too."

"Well, Harry." Stephanie had never called him "Harry" before. "It looks like you're going to have to decide if you'd rather be miserable with her or without her."

On Monday morning, during Harrison's telephone hour, Sharon buzzed him. "Felicia on line one."

He picked up the phone.

"Hi, Harrison. I'm trying to reach Carrie. The Bayou Buzzards want to change their name to Sloe Gin Fizz and I wondered what she thought."

Harrison drew a deep breath. "Carrie is no longer working for Rothwell."

"I know that. She's working at some day care center she researched for you, but I don't have the number and her answering machine isn't on."

Typical Carrie, Harrison thought, forgetting to turn on her machine. "I'll see that she gets your message," he said.

After hanging up the phone, he stared at it. Carrie was working at a day care center. One she'd visited for him.

You have to decide if you'd rather be miserable with her, or without her.

Slowly he opened the file with the names of the centers. According to Felicia, Carrie was at one of them.

"Misery loves company," he said to himself, and started dialing.

He found her at the fourth one he tried.

"Sharon, cancel my afternoon schedule," he said as he passed by her desk. "I don't know when I'll be returning."

Harrison was made to wait in the director's office, more nervous than he'd ever been in his life.

What if Carrie refused to see him? He wouldn't blame her. The past couple of weeks had made him see what life without Carrie would be like. He was in love with her, not in spite of her disorganization, but because of it.

Carrie wouldn't be Carrie otherwise.

The door opened and she walked in. "Hi," she said quietly.

Harrison's heart started beating in slow thuds. "Hi, yourself." Gone was the fashionably funky woman. She was wearing a sweater and a skirt and—he peered down—loafers. "You look like a schoolgirl."

"Because that's what I am. I've enrolled in summer classes to study early childhood education." She smiled. "I finally figured out what I was meant to do with my life and I have you to thank for it."

"You're welcome. What is it?"

"Working with young children. I love working here. When I visited that day..." Her voice trailed off, but she didn't need to finish. Harrison remembered the day all too well.

"It feels so right—the sort of right I've been waiting to feel." She looked at him, waiting.

Harrison drew a deep breath, hoping that this time,

the right words would come. "I've been trying to feel right, too, but I can't. I don't like my life without you. I love you just as you are."

Her smile lit up her face. "I've always loved you the way you are, and I've always been willing to compromise, but you never, not once, were willing to make any compromises for me. So, I told myself that you would have to be the one to come to me. And, oh, Harrison, I'm organized now. Sort of. Anyway, you'd be proud. There's something about being with children that makes me feel centered and focused."

"I thought there would be children in your future. I'm hoping they'll be mine. I've missed you, Carrie."

She looked down. "I've missed you, too. I—I organized my apartment." Her words were barely above a whisper. "I threw away a lot of stuff."

"But not the gumbo pot."

Looking up, she grinned. "Never the gumbo pot."

Harrison took a step toward her. "I can live with the gumbo pot."

Carrie took a step toward him. "I'd like to donate my furniture to a women's shelter."

Harrison took her hand. "I think displaying your fast-food toys in shadow boxes would look perfect in a nursery."

Her eyes grew luminous. "I'm ready for matching dishes." Carrie took his other hand.

Pulling her into his arms, Harrison said, "I'm ready to repot all my plants in hand-crafted Mexican pottery."

Carrie laughed. "I'm ready to move in!"

"Are you ready to marry me?"

Carrie smiled her wide, Carrie smile, then tilted her lips toward his. "I'm ready."

At the monthly meeting of the White Oak Bayou Residents' Board

"The next item on the agenda is a request from Harrison Rothwell to approve his fiancée as a new resident." Mrs. Greenborough smiled at Harrison. "First, may I extend my congratulations to you?"

"Thank you," Harrison replied.

"Will you tell us about your fiancée?"

"Caryn is studying to become a teacher specializing in early childhood. She's currently working at a day care center and would ultimately like to work with companies to establish on site day care centers for their employees. She, in fact, set up the emergency day care facility in my own company."

"Very commendable." Mrs. Greenborough's approval was echoed by the others.

"She grew up in Houston and her parents live in Memorial Hollow."

"Lovely area. Well, she certainly sounds like she'll be an asset to the White Oak Community. Is she here, now?"

Harrison shook his head. "She's coming directly from work and will be late."

"We look forward to meeting her. All those in favor of approving Mr. Rothwell's request to grant residency approval for his fiancée, please say 'aye.'"

"Aye," said the other board members.

"It's unanimous and Mr. Rothwell's request is approved." Mrs. Greenborough smiled. "I wish our next order of business was as pleasant.'' She moved Carrie's file in front of her. ''The next item on the agenda is Carrie Brent's appeal of her eviction.''

Mrs. Greenborough scanned the audience. ''As Ms. Brent does not appear to be in attendance, would you care to speak on her behalf, Mr. Rothwell?''

''I still believe we need to apply our rules equally, or not at all. In Carrie's case, I feel there was a deliberate campaign to break her lease.''

''Do any of the other members agree with Mr. Rothwell?''

J.G. shook his head, as did the two other members of the board.

''I believe further discussion is unnecessary.'' Mrs. Greenborough looked at Harrison, but he remained silent. ''All in favor of upholding the eviction, signify by saying 'aye.'''

Five ''ayes'' sounded.

''Opposed?''

Silence.

''Mr. Rothwell?''

''I voted in favor.''

Startled, Mrs. Greenborough continued, ''Well, then Carrie Brent's lease is terminated and she has thirty days to vacate the premises.'' Wearing an expression of satisfaction, she closed Carrie's file.

A dark-haired woman walked in the door and slipped into the back row. Harrison gave her a thumbs-up sign.

''You're too late, Miss Brent. Your appeal has been denied.''

''Oh, good,'' Carrie said. ''Now I won't have to forfeit my deposit.''

Mrs. Greenborough's face reddened. "You have been nothing but a troublemaker and I am looking forward to you leaving us."

"She's not leaving," Harrison said. He stood and gestured for Carrie to join him. "Mrs. Greenborough and members of the board, I'd like to present my fiancée—to whom you have recently granted residency—Caryn Brent."

Carrie grinned. "You can call me Carrie."

EPILOGUE

Two-thirty a.m.—six years later

CARRIE nudged him. "Brent's crying. It's your turn to get up."

"Tell me again when they're supposed to sleep all the way through the night?"

Carrie laughed sleepily. "He's probably teething."

Harrison remembered his son's fussiness over the last several nights. "There's no probably about it." He swung his feet over the edge of the bed, then stopped. Something about the crying was different. "That's not Brent. It's Stacy."

Carrie shot to a sitting position. "I've been expecting this."

"What? Expecting what?"

Illuminated by the hallway night-light, she shrugged into his favorite bathrobe—the fuzzy one that made her so huggable. "Nearly all the kids in her preschool have come down with colds during the past two weeks."

"Maybe she just had a bad dream," Harrison suggested hopefully.

Carrie was already out the door.

"Or maybe not," he mumbled and followed her. In matters dealing with their son and daughter, Carrie was usually right.

Harrison reached his daughter's bedroom just as Carrie switched on the bedside lamp.

"What's wrong sweetie?" Carrie pushed the light brown hair off Stacy's forehead.

"I had a bad *dreeeeeam!*" Stacy wailed.

"She's not hot," Carrie said as she gathered Stacy to her.

Well, how about that? He was right for once. Harrison quietly crossed the hall into Brent's room and slid the rocking chair out, putting it into Stacy's room.

Bundling Stacy into a blanket, Carrie settled into the rocker as the four-year-old whimpered about her dream.

"Sounds like you need my magic nightmare chasing potion," Harrison said. "Would you like that?"

With her lower lip sticking out, Stacy nodded. "Yes, Daddy."

Carrie smiled at him, love and approval shining from her eyes.

Feeling a lot better about being awakened, Harrison went to the kitchen to warm a cup of milk onto which he sprinkled a little cinnamon sugar. He'd invented the "magic potion" in desperation one night. Living with Carrie had taught him to be more creative.

Returning to the bedroom, he gave Stacy the cup, then sat on her bed watching as Carrie rocked her. He loved watching Carrie with their children. How incredibly lucky he was that she'd come into his life—and had drawn him into hers.

When Stacy finished the milk, Carrie kissed her on the forehead and Harrison was reminded of the night he'd fallen in love with her as she'd cared for Nathan.

Then he'd imagined they would have a curly-haired child with the Rothwell smile.

Stacy and her brother had his hair and Carrie's smile, but he was struck by how everything else was almost as he'd imagined it. Carrie was a terrific mother and as active as he'd thought she'd be. In fact, her Filofax was more detailed than his was. She'd also forced him to be much more of a hands-on father than he'd envisioned. And he liked it.

Life was less structured, but life was good.

And he wouldn't have it any other way.

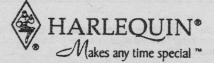

Take 2 bestselling love stories FREE

Plus get a FREE surprise gift!

Special Limited-Time Offer

Mail to Harlequin Reader Service®

3010 Walden Avenue
P.O. Box 1867
Buffalo, N.Y. 14240-1867

YES! Please send me 2 free Harlequin Romance® novels and my free surprise gift. Then send me 6 brand-new novels every month, which I will receive months before they appear in bookstores. Bill me at the low price of $2.90 each plus 25¢ delivery and applicable sales tax if any*. That's the complete price, and a saving of over 10% off the cover prices—quite a bargain! I understand that accepting the books and gift places me under no obligation ever to buy any books. I can always return a shipment and cancel at any time. Even if I never buy another book from Harlequin, the 2 free books and the surprise gift are mine to keep forever.

116 HEN CH66

Name	(PLEASE PRINT)
Address	Apt. No.
City	State Zip

This offer is limited to one order per household and not valid to present Harlequin Romance® subscribers. *Terms and prices are subject to change without notice. Sales tax applicable in N.Y.

UROM-98

DEBBIE MACOMBER

invites you to the

HEART OF TEXAS

Join Debbie Macomber as she brings you the lives and loves of the folks in the ranching community of Promise, Texas.

If you loved Midnight Sons—don't miss Heart of Texas! A brand-new six-book series from Debbie Macomber.

Available in February 1998 at your favorite retail store.

Heart of Texas by Debbie Macomber

Lonesome Cowboy	February '98
Texas Two-Step	March '98
Caroline's Child	April '98
Dr. Texas	May '98
Nell's Cowboy	June '98
Lone Star Baby	July '98

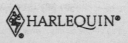

HARLEQUIN®

HPHRT1

♫Harlequin Romance®

Coming Next Month

#3515 THE DIAMOND DAD Lucy Gordon
Garth had promised his wife diamonds for their tenth anniversary—
Faye didn't want diamonds, she wanted a divorce! But with two gorgeous
children and his beautiful wife at stake, Garth was determined to do all
he could to save his family!

The Big Event! *One special occasion—that changes your life forever.*

#3516 HEAVENLY HUSBAND Carolyn Greene
It seemed incredible, but when Kim's ex-fiancé Jerry woke from his
accident he seemed like a totally different man. Instead of a womanizing
workaholic, he'd become the perfect hero. He said she was in danger,
and that she needed his protection. But the only danger Kim could
foresee was that maybe heaven *was* missing an angel—and they'd want
him back!

Guardian Angels: *Falling in love sometimes needs a little help from
above!*

#3517 THE TROUBLE WITH TRENT! Jessica Steele
When Trent de Havilland waltzed into Alethea's life, she was already
wanting to leave home. So Trent's idea that she move in with him could
have been the ideal solution. But Alethea's trouble with Trent wasn't so
much that she was living with him, but that she was falling in love with
him!

Look out also for another great **Whirlwind Weddings** title:

#3518 THE MILLION-DOLLAR MARRIAGE Eva Rutland
Tony Costello only found out about his bride's fortune after their
whirlwind romance had ended in a trip to the altar. He couldn't forgive
her for being rich and for keeping it a secret. Melody had deliberately
tried to conceal her true worth for the sake of Tony's pride; now she
would have to fight to save their marriage. Rich or poor, she loved
Tony—she was just going to have to prove it!

Whirlwind Weddings: *who says you can't hurry love?*